Inspector Loop Visits America

Inspector Loop Visits America

Danny B. Lamont

ARPress LLC
45 Dan Road Suite 5
Canton MA 02021
Hotline: 1(888) 821-0229
Fax: 1(508) 545-7580

Ordering Information:
Quantity sales. Special discounts are available on quantity purchases by corporations, associations, and others. For details, contact the publisher at the address above.

Printed in the United States of America.

ISBN-13: Softcover   979-8-89330-116-8
               eBook   979-8-89330-117-5

Library of Congress Control Number: 2024901466

Contents

CHAPTER ONE

To the south of London, over the gently rolling farmlands of wheat and barley, past the picturesque pastures of sheep, and the many hedgerows which separate them, are the two peaceful villages of Larger Elfinwood and Crushed Eastwich. A quiet country road known as Ridge Ending Lane winds its way past the hedgerows and through the woods from one village to the other.

About two kilometers outside of Larger Elfinwood, just past the Johnston sheep farm, is a large gap in the hedgerow. Here, a graveled driveway leads up to a small country estate known as Twinned Loop. A well-kept, two story, thatched roofed English cottage sits at the end of the winding drive. The whitewashed walls are covered with ivy. The many windows of the cottage are Tudor style and are set slightly out from the walls. Landscaped areas are placed around the house which allows the front cobblestone to walk to branch off and wander through and around the beds to the rear of the cottage. Low growing ground cover such as juniper mingled with nandinas and hollies for color are in these landscaped beds. At the end of the walk there is a walled garden with a thick oaken gate. Its ancient iron hinges and latch have been kept well-oiled over the centuries. A small forest is also part of the property and surrounds the yard, cottage, and gardens on three sides. There is a man working in the garden, who is busily pruning the hollies and junipers. He is an older man with hair that is turning white. This country gentleman is dressed in an older shirt, baggy pants, and old gardening shoes. To an outsider, who would see this cottage and its grounds for the first time, it would appear that this person must be the gardener; however, he would be very mistaken. His name is Ulnar Loop, but to everyone who knows him he is just an Inspector.

He was born Ulnar Lewis Loop on August 2, 1926, to a prominent and well to do family in London, England. His father and mother, Merlin and Morgana Loop, were both students of Sir Edward Richard Henry during the early years of the Science of Fingerprints; later Henry and the Loops became close friends. Of course, with Ulnar's name, which is the most common type of fingerprint patterns, he became very interested in science at an early age. Although his mother wanted him to become a Foreign Service Officer after he graduated from the University, it was not going to come true. Indeed, he followed in his father's footsteps just as everyone suspected he would. After he was hired by the Yard, his rise in rank, due to his ability, was rapid. He soon became a well-known teacher and aided other young people who were finding their way through the mysteries of fingerprints.

The Inspector has just recently retired from Scotland Yard, after almost fifty years of outstanding service; where, during that time, he became the foremost authority on the Science of Fingerprints in the world. As a result of his outstanding service to Her Majesty's Government, he was given this small estate by a grateful Queen and Country. Much of his work is sealed under the Official Secrets Act and will not become public knowledge for at least fifty years. It can be said, however, that he saved not only England, but many other countries from unnecessary violence because of his work in this forensic science.

As he trimmed his bushes on this beautiful June afternoon, he felt at peace. He also felt uncomfortable with this quiet country life which has been so different from the intense concentration and challenge that filled his days as the senior man in his fingerprint laboratory at the Yard. Suddenly, he placed his hands on his lower back and straightened up while he stayed in a kneeling position. This brought about a good-sized number of snaps, crackles, and pops from his back. ''I'm beginning to sound like an American breakfast cereal'', he muttered to himself. While in this position, he heard a faint sound, almost like the sound of a bell that has been carried on the light breeze. Apparently, he had not heard this sound earlier because of his work with the hollies. The

Inspector stayed in this position and listened even closer to the sound. "Yes", he whispered to himself, "that is definitely a bell, and I know just who it belongs to."

He got to his feet, brushed the loose soil from the knees of his trousers, and slowly walked back up the cobblestone path. He went back through the garden gate, latching it behind him, to the back wall of the cottage. There, Ulnar bent over an outdoor spigot, turned on the water, and washed the dirt off his hands. He turned off the faucet, and taking his time, he walked around to the front of the house to the point where the cobblestone walkway joined the driveway. With his arms folded in front of him, he waited for his visitor to arrive.

His soon to arrive company was only about 200 yards from the Inspector's home and was still rapidly ringing the bell on his bike. His legs pumped the pedals as fast as his thirty-five year old knees would allow. Suddenly, there was a break in the hedgerow which announced the entrance to Ulnar's home. Constable Erin Correy, the owner of the knees and the bicycle barely kept his balance as his transportation threatened to dump him onto the graveled drive. With a quick twist of the handlebars and a good deal of muttering under his breath he managed to stay upright, thus saving his pride, and started to slow down to a stop in front of Inspector Loop. Breathing hard, he got off the bike and walked on rubbery legs towards the Inspector. At the same time, he brought up his right hand to the peak of his helmet in a casual salute. Ulnar met him halfway with his right hand extended in greeting.

"Good afternoon, Constable", he said while shaking hands. "Granted, it is a beautiful day to be out riding, but you should take more care and slow down. After all, your wife would never forgive me if you should have a heart attack or fall off of that thing you are riding and break your neck. She's too wonderful a lady to be left as a grieving widow."

"Yes, you're quite right, Inspector", he replied as he dropped his hand to his side. "But, I haven't a choice in the matter. There was an important phone call for you at the station in London. Of course, if you had a phone here at Twinned Loop, then whenever somebody wanted to get in touch, they could ring you directly."

"Quite true, Constable, quite true. I really should; however, then I would have to put up with a considerable amount of nonsense from people trying to sell me all sorts of gimmicks and such. After all, I have been retired for nearly a year now, and no one of consequence has tried to contact me. So, to receive one now is rather surprising. Can you tell me who it is that called?"

"I'm sorry sir, but I'm under orders not to discuss it; except to say, that it is important. And that you are to accompany me to the station and call a certain number."

"Certainly, Constable", replied Ulnar, "Just let me clean up a little bit and change into some respectable clothes. It wouldn't look right, being arrested for looking like a tramp; especially when I'm going back to the station with you. Would you care for a cup of tea while you wait?"

Without waiting for a reply, Ulnar turned and proceeded up the cobblestone walk followed by Constable Correy. They entered the cottage. Before washing up, Ulnar Loop escorted the constable into his library and fixed him a cup of tea. While he was upstairs, he started thinking about what Constable Correy had said about the phone call, which was absolutely nothing. The mysteriousness of the situation disturbed Ulnar. But he decided to wait until they were on their way to the station in Larger Ellinwood before he questioned Erin any more on the subject.

Are you ready to leave now, Constable", asked the Inspector as he came down the stairs.

"Yes sir, I am."

Ulnar went around to the garage on the other side of the cottage, and after a few moments, got the Bentley to start. It seemed that the car had a mind of its own; when he needed it to start, it balked. When it didn't matter, well, there wasn't a problem. He pulled the motor car around to the front of the cottage and stopped but left the motor running. With Erin's help, he put the bicycle into the boot of the Bentley and started to drive back to the village of Larger Ellinwood. It was a somewhat longer drive than Constable Erin Correy expected. Ulnar Loop needed some time to talk with him.

"Erin", he said, 'Please understand that I am only trying to find out what is going on. I just do not understand the need for all of this secrecy. Are you certain that you cannot shed any further light on this matter."

"Inspector, I only wish that I could. But you'll just have to accept my original statement", Erin replied.

The Inspector pulled his car off to the side of Ridge Ending Lane and pulled on the emergency brake. He turned to his left and faced the Constable. He was beginning to seriously dislike what was happening to him, and he meant to get to the bottom of it.

"What do you mean?" he inquired sharply.

"What I mean, Inspector, is that I can't answer your question. I'm under orders from the Yard and the Home Office, not too. And yes, before you ask, Sergeant Sanderson and I placed several calls after the original one to us, to make sure that it wasn't a prank. You're liked too much by us and we don't want to see you hurt. So, you'll have to ask those questions to the appropriate authority."

"All right Constable, I will do just that. And thank you for your concern for my privacy", he added in a nicer tone. With that said, and obviously nothing more to be gained by trying to blow beat Erin, the Inspector released the hand break, turned the steering wheel to the right, pulled back onto the lane, and proceeded into the village.

When they approached the station, Sergeant Sanderson heard the vehicle turn onto the loose stone that served as a parking area in front and stepped outside to watch the Bentley being parked. When he reached it, he opened Constable Correy's door and told him to go inside. The sergeant, who took the original call, was aware of the problems that Erin might have run into when he visited the Inspector.

As if the sergeant were speaking to a solicitor, he said coldly to Ulnar, "Inspector, if you will follow me I will give you the number that you will need to ring up the Yard. And from what London had to say earlier, all of your questions should be answered." With that, the sergeant led the way into the two story, red brick building that served as the Constables' station for Larger Elfinwood and the surrounding area. When they entered the structure, Ulnar Loop went over to the phone and dialed the London exchange and then the number for New Scotland Yard. After just two rings the receiver on the other end was picked up.

''New Scotland Yard, Welsley speaking."

''Welsley, this is Inspector Ulnar Loop, formerly of the Yard speaking, please put me through to the Commander".

"One moment, sir", he replied.

"This is Commander Cummings."

"Commander, this is Ulnar Loop. I understand that you needed to interrupt my retirement to speak to me on some mysterious matter."

The Commander of the Criminal Identification Center of Scotland Yard agreed that it was not only important, but that Inspector Ulnar Loop was the only person that could be of service.

"I do not like disturbing your retirement in this manner, but you are the most experienced person that I know in fingerprints", the Commander said, "And it is because of this ability that you are being ordered to travel to America and look at some new technology. This order, of course, comes from the highest authority."

"I understand that, but it was agreed upon at the time of my retirement, that because of my work on the: fingerprint evidence from the Irish bombings, and some other work, I would not be bothered."

''Normally", replied to the Commander, "That would be a given, but something new has come along and this organization needs your assistance with it. In point of fact, Her Majesty has personally ordered you to accept or lose your benefits."

"Commander, since you have put it that way," responded the Inspector, "I will listen to what you have to say."

"Good. Now listen very carefully, and you are not to repeat this to an ... "

"Yes, I know, another soul, or it will result in my not working anywhere in the entire free world if I repeat what you are about to tell me to anyone. Paul, you give me no choice. I will accept." This part of the conversation took a few minutes; after which, Ulnar listened to the instructions that his old friend and student had to give to him.

"Ulnar, this is a sensitive subject, and I will not downplay it. In the colonies, that is the United States, the Federal Bureau of investigation has not only started a new computer program, but it has also moved part of its fingerprint identification operations to another state. Believe it or not, the Americans have gotten somewhat intelligent and taken part of this massive law enforcement agency and moved it outside of the Nuclear Bomb Area.

"So, what does this have to do with a very retired person like me, Paul?"

"Ulnar, I will read you the official order: 'By Order of Her Majesty, Elizabeth II, Queen of England, that Inspector Ulnar Lewis Loop on behalf of New Scotland Yard, will proceed with all possible speed to the United States. In particular, The Federal Bureau of Investigation, and there he will visit the new facilities in Clarksburg, West Virginia. After his inspection of this scientific compound, he will make any recommendations that are necessary for the stabilization, growth, and continuation of the newly vested National Identification Center, which is to be built in the Kensington district of London.'"

The Inspector knew that he had no choice but to obey this order. So, without any further argument, he simply said, "Brother John, thank you. Goodbye."

The Inspector rang off and took a deep breath. He turned around and walked through a doorway that led into the office that Sergeant Sanderson and Constable Corney shared. A deep, thick silence descended in the office with only unasked questions showing on the faces of the two officers. Ulnar did not help by answering them; instead, he bid them a good day, turned slowly around, and like a man in a trance, walked out of the station to his motor car. He slid behind the wheel and carefully drove away from the building. He headed for the town's only car hire firm. After making arrangements for the following morning, he drove home, packed his clothes for the trip, had a light supper, and retired early. He knew that the next day would start very early.

The next day, just as the sun came up, Ulnar got up and performed his morning chores. By the time that he finished, the hired car appeared. Its wheels crunched on the gravel, in front of the cottage. The driver helped him load his luggage into the car. As the car pulled out of the drive, the Inspector softly said, "To the train station, please." These are the only words that are spoken during the entire trip to the depot. Once there, he paid the driver, checked his bags with the porter, and boarded the London bound train.

When he arrived in the city, he promptly hailed a cab and went to the Yard to pick up his travel voucher, letter of introduction, and expense money. Finally, he arrived at Heathrow Airport got on the British Airways Concord that would fly him to the United States. All of this was done automatically.

CHAPTER TWO

"**A**s he settled back in his seat to await take off, he accepted a pillow from the flight attendant. Thanking her, he turned his head so that he could look out the window. Shortly after takeoff, with only the thought of how fast this change in his retirement had happened, he fell into a fitful sleep. He did not realize that this trip was about to change his life in a much larger way.

"Traveling at Mach One, makes the flight from England to the United States seem very short when compared to a regular one; so, before the Inspector knew it, he was landing at Dulles International Airport which is just south of Washington D. C. Just inside the passenger terminal was a Scotland Yard liaison officer from the British Embassy. When he saw Ulnar Loop enter the area, he stepped forward to greet him. "Good afternoon, Inspector; I'm Geoffrey Cambridge from the embassy. To make it easier on you, you may call me Geoff."

""Thank you Geoff, it's a pleasure to meet you", he replied. "I do have one question though. How did you know me? A picture perhaps, or", he added, chuckling, "Did they send you my fingerprints?"

""Neither sir. You taught a class on forensic sciences some ten years ago, and I've not forgotten that class, or you."

""Ten years, well that was some time ago."

""Yes, it was sir; shall we go?" Geoff said as he escorted the Inspector towards the luggage pickup and then to the customs area. Here, Mr. Cambridge showed his identification to the customs agents and passed on through to the Inspector. Outside the terminal, he showed Ulnar to an official embassy staff car which was illegally parked in a handicapped spot. "Is there anything else I can do for you?" He asked.

""Thank you", Ulnar Loop replied. "But getting me through customs and giving me a lift to catch my train is indeed more than enough help." They drove off in the embassy vehicle for that long ride to downtown D.C.

""Sorry, sir, but there has been a slight change in plans. It seems that because of the time of day, and the fact that the new Director of the FBI wishes to meet you before you travel to their new Identification Building, we have secured sleeping quarters for you. You will be delayed but one day. These orders came through my superior from Commander Cummings."

""Very well. It seems that the Commander is going to make the most out of the interruption of my retirement." Then hesitantly, 'Wait a minute. Did you say through your superior? Who are you with, Geoff?"

""Oh, sorry about that. I'm with the Anti-Terrorist Branch of the Yard."

""Well, with that mouthful, and the fact that you remember a class I conducted ten years ago, how could I resist?"

"Soon, they drove through the front gate of the British Embassy, and Inspector Loop was conducted to Ambassador Ambrose's Office. They exchanged greetings, and the ambassador invited Ulnar to join him for a cup of tea. During this time, it is explained that a letter of introduction would be given to him in the morning before he went to the J. Edgar Hoover Building to meet with the Director.

""Thank you very much Ambassador. By the way, I understand that your staff has arranged a room for me." Ulnar said.

""Yes, they have. A car will take you there after dinner, that is if you will join me, and we will have it pick you up in the morning."

"The Inspector graciously accepted the invitation to dine with the Ambassador. It was a somewhat private dinner as those types of things go in embassies. There were only the Ambassador, his family, and the top officials. The Inspector came alive during the meal. This was not hard for him to do because of all the compliments and praises that were heaped upon him. In fact, as the dinner wore on, his stories started to drift slightly away from the absolute truth. More to the point, some of them became very tall tales. While everyone was listening to these flights of fancy, and then trying to outdo each other, the Inspector wondered why he has drifted away from other people, to almost become a recluse at Twinned Loop.

"Finally, the dinner broke up, and the people started to leave for their own quarters. "Ambassador, thank you very much for the fine dinner and company", the Inspector said. Ambassador Ambrose told him that he was welcome and hoped that Ulnar would have a pleasant night's sleep. Mr. Loop was driven to his hotel in an Embassy car and escorted to his room by Geoffrey Cambridge. It was then that the day caught up with him. He unpacked his pajamas and such along with clothes that he would wear tomorrow to the FBI building. After he had called the desk to leave a wakeup call for 7:30 in the morning, he laid down. He was sound asleep before his head hit the pillow and did indeed have a pleasant night's sleep.

"RRRRIIIINNNNGGGG. RRRRIIIINNNNGGGG. This sound was trying to get through to the Inspector very early the next morning. Sleepily, he reached out with his right hand that, at the moment, seemed to belong to someone else and pawed at the telephone. Finally, after three tries, he managed to grab the receiver and in a morning croak type voice said into it, 'Hello?"

""Good Morning, sir", a bright, cheerful, and youthful voice boomed from the receiver. "It is now 7:30".

"Still croaking, the Inspector replied, "Thank you." After two tries, with that same uncoordinated hand, he successfully hung up the phone. Tiredly, he stumbled from the bed to the bathroom, and after a long, hot shower he felt partly human again. Dressing in his best suit, he wondered why on earth did he agreed to take this trip? After all, he could be at his cottage right now, working in his prize gardens. Where, over the past few months, he had found a pleasant peace. There have, up until the other day that is, been no disturbances. There were no visitors and no solicitors. No one from work clamoring for him to hurry. Hurry here and there-processing latent evidence, comparing that same evidence against some of the worst scum in Great Britain. Everyone was important, every case was equally important. There was now no single person or group of people wanting to do away with him because of his findings or his testimony. No, all of that was behind him now. Still, why had he decided to take this trip? For that matter, why had he treated so many of his friends so badly? He looked at himself in the mirror as he finished these thoughts and shook his head to clear the haze from his mind. "I'm just becoming an old fogy, that's all," he mumbled softly to himself. When he finished dressing, he looked at himself in the mirror once more. Then, more or less satisfied with what he saw, he turned to the door and opened it.

"And as he stepped through the doorway, he almost bounced back into the room. There, in front of him with his face turning to an embarrassed red, stood a very young and very serious man. "E ... eh ... excuse ... m ... m ... me, suh ... sir", he stammered. "Ahem, I didn't know that you were leaving so soon, sir", he said with a little more firmness.

""That's quite alright, young man", Ulnar replied. "I wasn't aware that someone was right outside my door. Especially one so much larger than myself. Next time I will be more cautious when I come out of a door." The Inspector hesitated a few moments and then looked at the young man again. "What are you doing here if you do not mind me asking?"

"""Sir, I'm ... that is ... we. We are here to make sure that you're safe and that you remain that way."

"

"Looking around the carpeted and narrow hallway, he asked, 'We?'"

"

""Yes, Inspector, we", he said with confidence, now that he was in control of himself again. "Harry, Smythe that is, and myself have been here all night. Oh, terribly sorry sir, I'm George Black. We're your protection this morning until you are picked up for your visit with the Director of the FBI."

""You seem to know a great deal about my business, George. Why is that? In fact, why do I need all of this protection?"

"

"George, more firmly, and with a bit of steel behind it, replied, "Inspector, we know, because we have to. Again, for your protection. The protection is by order of the Queen. I've seen the order, and those of us assigned to the Diplomatic Protection Service do not take our duties, lightly."

""You're right, Mr. Black. I don't know what came over me, must be jet lag; my apologies."

""Accepted, sir. Where is it that you're off to; Harry and I must know."

""I thought that a spot of breakfast would be just the thing to complete the waking up process. Would you two care to join me?"

""Thank you, no. We cannot do our job correctly if we're eating. But you go right ahead and enjoy yourself Oh, by the way, to finish the explanation, that is. There were rumors that one of the groups that you foiled so well, was possibly planning to end your life. At least, that is, according to our sources, and they are rarely wrong. Besides, as I said, it is by order of the Queen. And I'm not about to cross her, Inspector."

"Ulnar looked more closely into George's eyes, and there he saw a certain hardness that one so young should not have. It said that he, and probably Harry, had been to places and had had to do unpleasant things that must be done to protect the Crown. With respect he asked, "You, and your partner, were not perchance part of the Special Air Service at one time, were you?"

""Yes, we are. We're on special assignment to the embassy while you're here." And that was all that he would say on the subject.

"Ulnar strode down the hall and turned at the comer to go to the elevators. There, he saw Harry; he had been right with his assumption. He passed by this second young man and continued to the lift. While the three of them waited for one of the elevators to appear they completely ignored one another. When an elevator finally appeared, they rode it in silence to the first floor. They got off with George in front. He entered the dining room a few minutes before Ulnar, and Harry entered a couple of minutes later. The two of them took up positions at tables where they could watch the entire room and the entranceway.

"The Inspector ordered a small breakfast of juice, coffee, cereal, and toast, lightly buttered. While he ate, he reviewed the conversation with George. Why, he thought, am I acting like this? I never used to be this way; has retirement done this much damage to me? ''Well," he said softly to himself, "this has got to change. I'm acting absolutely balmy." After breakfast, he strolled out into the lobby, his feet whispering across the thick carpet, and sat down on one of the stuffed, uncomfortable hotel lobby chairs. There, he waited for his ride to the Hoover Building.

"He amused himself during this wait by trying to guess why the people who walked around him were really at the hotel, and what business did they had that could make them be in such a hunt. Harry and George were doing the same thing, but for different reasons. In fact, one person caught their eye; Harry was given the nod by George. He moved slowly and silently, so as not to give a warning, towards the stranger. Suddenly, he rushed the person and pushed him into a comer just past the elevators. No one could see from the lobby. ''What's your interest in the old gentleman?" he asked, nodding his head in the direction of the Inspector.

"''Nothing", replied to the stranger. ''I'm head of security for the hotel. We've had some problems with older men who are not registered here trying to bother the female guests. I thought that he might be another one of them."

Harry, who had to seriously restrain himself from laughing, showed his identification and said firmly, "That older gentleman is a guest in this country. If you'd like to start an international incident, then go ahead, and try to bother him. But rest assured that if you did, then the Queen of England would not be very happy, and your own President would be very unhappy. In fact, everyone over you would be the same way. Therefore, I can inform you of a very important fact, you will be extremely unhappy and more than likely, without a job for the rest of your natural life." With this said, Harry left the house detective, who was by now, literally shaking in his shoes. Harry resumed his previous position in the lobby.

About half an hour later, Geoffrey Cambridge came through the front doors, first looking left, and spotting George, then looking right, and spotting Harry. Then he looked straight ahead and saw Ulnar Loop. Nodding his head at the two men on loan to the Diplomatic Protection Service, he walked up to the Inspector. Harry and George quietly left the lobby and went outside to take up positions there.

"Good morning, Inspector", Geoff said in a bright, cheerful voice. "Did you have that good night's sleep?

Ulnar, hiding a grin, said, "Yes, I did, thank you. By the way, I apologize, and this is not the first one this morning, to you for my behavior yesterday. It seems that ever since the phone call to Commander Cummings, I've been behaving badly by biting every one's head off"

"Inspector, the Commander said that you would be acting that way when I talked to him yesterday. He also said that you would come around and be your normal likeable self in due time. In other words, accepted."

The Inspector got up from the chair and walked with a slight spring in his step for the first time during the trip. He went out the hotel door, across the busy, imitation cobble stone sidewalk, to the rear door of the embassy car. Geoffrey opened the door for him and closed it after he was completely inside. He then opened the front passenger door and slid in next to the driver and closed the door. Once the car pulled away from the comer, it was immediately bogged down in the late morning rush hour traffic that is so common in Washington, D.C. It did not seem to move for at least ten minutes. The cars and buses, the latter belching black, bad-smelling fumes, moved no more than twenty yards at a time, and that was when there was a large break in the traffic.

"Good grief, I thought that London traffic was impossible, but this is ridiculous", said the Inspector.

""It is quite something to see, I agree", said Geoff "One thing is to read about it or to be told about it before you're stationed here, but to experience it is another thing altogether. In fact, Inspector, it's as if the traffic is a living, breathing life organism that wants to get your hopes up with a little break in the traffic pattern, before it crushes those hopes beneath its wheels with a very grim reality."

"They rode on in silence. After a while they came to a comer and turned left towards Pennsylvania Avenue. The traffic was still very bad. Geoff broke the silence, "I heard from the man I replaced that it could get worse."

""Worse than this", asked Ulnar? "I don't believe that for one minute."

""Yes. It seems that during the winter, when the snow comes, this town almost comes to a complete stop. They say that getting out, if it snows on a workday, could take you hours. As a matter of fact, he told me about the time that a storm hit that day the plane crashed just after taking off from the National Airport. A number of streets were closed because of the storm and others because of the crash. Besides that, one of the subway trains derailed and caused even more problems by shutting down some of the larger and busier lines. It's my understanding that a normal hour and a half drive home took closer to five hours."

"Completely shocked, the Inspector said, "Incredible! How did the people manage?"

""Not easily I understand. Oh", Geoffrey said after they turned left onto Pennsylvania Avenue, "There's those concrete posts in front of the White House that you must have heard about. Ugly things, if you ask me, but they do the job that they were designed to do, which is to keep any potential car bomber from doing his mad act of destruction.

"Directly across the street you can see Lafayette Park with all of its different protestors; that building just before the park is the Blair House---that's where they put up visiting heads of state that have official business to conduct with the President and his Cabinet."

"Ulnar sat quietly in the back seat of the embassy vehicle while taking in all of these sights. On the next block, on the same side of Pennsylvania Avenue as the President's Residence, he saw the Executive Office Building, where President Truman had his offices because of work being done at the White House. It is also where the Vice President performs his duties. Because of that concentration, he was taken by complete surprise when the driver suddenly started to make a series of turns after they passed these buildings. Apparently because of a small park that was in the way. "Do these tiny little squares of grass and statues interfere with the traffic very often?" he asked breathlessly.

""Inspector, you would be very surprised at how many of these pocket-sized parks there are in the district. And they're not only little squares; there is one that is a huge traffic circle consisting of some six lanes. Depending on which lane you're in will depend on which street you will end up on. It's like a large macadam and concrete spider web, but to fully understand it you would have to be caught up in it."

"Ulnar leaned back into the well-padded, and very comfortable, rear seat and continued to look out the windows at the many buildings. Some of which appeared to imitate Roman, or Grecian, architecture, with their pillars and sculptures. On his left he saw the National Theater; then on his right he saw the Washington Monument, which took so long to build and is still not finished according to the original plans. Looking straight ahead he saw the Capitol Building, sitting on a small rise of land. It's bright, white dome and columns shining radiantly in the midmorning sun. Then, across the street from the Justice Building, he got his first glimpse of the J. Edgar Hoover Building. "Good night! Is that where we're going?"

""Yes, it is. Impressive, isn't it?" Geoffrey said with some humor.

"Ulnar said, "That's one description. It looks more like a modem version of a massive fortress or a concrete block house from the war. Well, Ludwig the Mad does meet Frank Lloyd Wright. If the government had built something like that in England, the riots would have been so bad that they would make the coal strikes look like a Boy Scout Jamboree." With that said, the embassy car turned left onto Tenth Street. About halfway up the block, in the center of the Hoover Building, there was an opening. They turned right and went down the slight slope to the guard. The driver stopped the car and handed out Geoff's and his identification. "Here's our credentials; our names and Inspector Ulnar Loop's should be on your list."

""They are", said the guard. "Please proceed down the ramp to the first level. That's the VIP area. I'll call upstairs and have somebody meet you there."

""Thank you."

"They drove down the ramp to the place that the guard had pointed out. The driver pulled the car into a marked VIP parking slot, put the car in park, and turned off the engine. Geoffrey Cambridge opened his door and got out of the car. He went back to the rear passenger door and opened it. Ulnar had just stepped out when the two of them were joined by a third person.

""Good morning, gentlemen; I'm Special Agent Samantha Adams", she said as she stretched out her right hand.

""Good morning, Agent Adams", Geoffrey replied, shaking her hand. He introduced her to the Inspector. "This is Inspector Ulnar Loop, formerly of Scotland Yard."

""It's a pleasure to meet you, Inspector", she said offering her hand to him.

""Thank you Agent Adams", he replied, also taking her hand.

""If you gentlemen will come with me, I'll take you to Director Dickinson's office", she said as she started to lead the way to the elevators. As the two men started to follow her, Geoff turned to the driver and told him to stay with the car. Although they both knew that the vehicle was safe in this part of the building, the prime rules were always followed. It was simple; regardless of the place, an embassy car must never be left unattended. After all, lives depended on this rule being obeyed.

"When the three of them reached the bank of elevators, there was one waiting; they got on. Agent Adams said, "Seven, please", to the agent operating the device. When it reached the seventh floor, they got off and walked around a bend to a hallway. The three law enforcement personnel followed it up to the far northeast comer of the building. They entered the outer office of the Director of the Federal Bureau of Investigation. Agent Samantha Adams told the private secretary, ''Please let the Director know that Inspector Ulnar Loop and ... ," she raised her eye brows and looked up at Geo

""Geoffrey Cambridge of Scotland Yard and the Inspector's bodyguard," he said.

"She nodded at the secretary who finished the announcement and said, "Please go right in." The man from Scotland Yard and the Inspector entered the office while Special Agent Samantha Adams sat down in a government vinyl sofa and picked up a month-old magazine to pass the time.

"The office was quite large with two of the walls being made entirely of glass. Framed in the V of the walls was a large oak desk; the floors were carpeted in muted shades of gray and white of good quality. In the comer opposite the Director's desk was a conversation area made up of a few leather chairs and a sofa. The two glass walls offered an excellent view of much of downtown Washington including RFK Stadium, the Smithsonian Castle, the Lincoln Memorial and beyond those, the haze of Northern Virginia. Also behind the immense desk was Director Charles Dickinson, who got up from his custom-made chair; he walked around the left side of his desk and warmly greeted his two visitors. "Good morning, Inspector, Mr. Cambridge," he said while shaking their hands in the tum. "It's a privilege to finally meet you, Inspector. I've heard quite a bit about you over the years, not to mention the articles you have published on some of your larger cases. I didn't really know if my request through your ambassador to meet you would be granted or not until yesterday evening. Please, gentlemen, have a seat," he said while motioning his arm towards the sofa and chairs.

"As Ulnar and Geoffrey took their seats, Director Dickinson went back to his desk. He leaned over it and spoke into the intercom to his secretary, Miriam Mims. ''Mrs. Mims, would you see if you can rustle up some tea for our guests?" Softly, he added, "And be sure that it is my English Tea and not that awful stuff that GSA has been trying to pawn off on us."

"Geoff spoke up, "Thank you sir, none for me."

"Looking back over his shoulder the Director said, "Sorry, please make that for two, instead."

"'I'd be glad to, Director."

""Thank you."

"He went back across the room and sat down on one of the chairs facing the sofa where Ulnar was sitting. Geoffrey Cambridge remained standing off to one side so that he could keep an eye on not only Ulnar, but on the entrance to the office as well. The Director sat back in the leather chair and crossed his legs. When he was comfortable, he said, ''Well, Inspector ... "

""Please Director, just make it Ulnar."

""'Very well then, Ulnar it is." I'm curious as to how you became interested in the Science of Fingerprints? Obviously, it was the perfect choice, but there must have been a powerful reason for it."

"Chuckling a little, the Inspector said, "Actually, it was more an accident of birth than anything that was planned. With the last name of Loop, and with my father and mother not only good personal friends of Sir Edward Henry, but also involved with science themselves, there could be no other outcome. And to cap it all off, they named me Ulnar."

""I understand about your last name, but what did being named Ulnar have to do with it?" Sorry, but I was a street agent and what little bit I knew about: fingerprints was lost years ago."

""A loop is the most common type of :fingerprint pattern. There are two types of loops, radial and ulnar. A radial loop slants towards the radius bone, or the thumb; while the ulnar loop slants towards the ulna bone or the little finger. So with that particular, or rather peculiar, name, and with :fingerprints being the major profession in the family, I had no choice in the matter. Of course, when I grew older I started studying the subject. I soon found, for whatever reason, that I also had a knack for it. Being a late child, my parents were retired by the time I went to the University; however, they still helped me a great deal, and they paved my way into the Yard. The rest as you Americans say, is history."

""I'm not trying to be nosy, but I am curious about your parents' names."

"" 'Yes, most people are. But they have a right to be. After all, most parents are not named Merlin and Morgana. The way it was described to me by my mother, when she thought I was old enough to understand, is that she was named after the sorceress, Morgana. Her parents believed that as pretty as she was when she was born, she would put a spell on any man that she wanted. This was, no doubt, wishful thinking on their part.

"My father, it appears, was born into a family of scientists, with his father being a professor of chemistry. I believe that my mother said that his parents were both taken with King Arthur and the stories of that time period. Because everyone on that side of the family was into one science or another, then it held to reason that my father would, also. But he would also be a real wizard at whatever field of science he went into. That is how he became to be named Merlin. It didn't really matter, though. The two of them met at Scotland Yard when they were both starting out in fingerprints. And, of course, with those names, they had to get married.

"Although mother was never very clear on this, his parents apparently did not expect him to go into a science that had no real backing. And neither did her's. They were all believers in Alfonse Bertillon's work with the measurements of the body. Fingerprints were too new. Of course, when the Yard started its files using the newly adopted Henry system of classification, and after it proved to be a very accurate science, then they had no problem with their children working in the science. And so, it was there that my mother and father met and later got married, with Sir Edward being the best man."

""That's quite a story," the Director said as he poured more tea for the two of them. "What was your first big case that you handled," he asked as he settled back into his chair.

""That would have been right after I was put in charge of the processing laboratory. Although I was still comparing latent impressions, and teaching, I was working now with those people who process the latent prints at crime scenes and taking other items back to the laboratory to process them with chemicals. It was in the middle seventies, and there was an arsonist, who of course, liked to set fires. He always used a full five-liter petrol can. This fire bug, as you would call him, would place the can in a paper sack, leave it where he wanted to set his fire after he set his timer. When the fire was put out, there would be very little left in the way of evidence. This was happening all over the countryside. Finally, the local authorities called us in.

"I went to the scene with two of my people from the lab. We found the petrol can severely burned and no real hope of any latent impressions being left. However, on lifting the can up we found a small piece of the paper sack which had no fire damage because the petrol can was on top of it. Carefully, we took it back to a small mobile lab we had set up and soaked it in a chemical called Ninhydrin; this reacts to the amino acids found in sweat. After drying and adding a little humidity to the piece of sack, a partial palmprint was developed from where the suspect carried the petrol can. Later, when a suspect was developed, we compared the latent palmprint with the inked palmprints that we took of the subject. They matched; he went to trial in the Old Bailey and was found guilty.

""I remember that now, it was in a piece written at the time of your retirement. It also mentioned the Libyan Embassy shoot out."

" There's really very little to that. I was called because I was working in the lab and doing some crime scene work. After the Libyans closed their embassy and left, the Yard went over the room that the firing came from to look for shell casings. We knew that they would take the automatic weapons with them along with the brass casings. We were just hoping that they erred. Of course, they did. After searching the room, with no results; I suggested that we undo the ties on the heavy drapes. When this was done, the drapes smoothed straight, and then shaken out, several shell casings fell to the floor that had been caught up in those folds."

""This did not help with their opinion of you."

""No, it did not, and because of their terrorist activities, I've had several run ins with the scurvy lot.

""So now they have a death warrant out for you."

""Which is the reason for me being here," Geoffrey Cambridge said from where he was standing.

"Certainly, they would not try to strike him here, in America; there are better targets I'm sure," replied Director Dickinson.

"Perhaps, sir, but we're not taking any chances; by "we" Inspector, I mean the Queen and the Prime Minister as well," he added for Ulnar's sake along with a very serious expression.

""Point taken, Geoffrey, point well taken," replied Ulnar.

"The Director looked at his watch as Ulnar and Geoffrey were discussing his safety. "Inspector, Mr. Cambridge, because of the time, would you do me the honor of joining me for lunch?"

"The other two exchanged looks with one another. Then Ulnar said, "We'd be delighted to."

The three of them left Dickinson's office, and after a brief word to Special Agent Adams, they continued through the outer office. They turned left in the hallway and walked to the elevators. They took one down to the cafeteria. Upon entering the cafeteria, they went back to an area reserved for the Director, his immediate assistants, and his distinguished guests. The three of them went directly to a small buffet that had been set up.

Charles chose a small salad because of his diet. Ulnar and Geoff both took a meat dish along with a small salad, as these items looked to be halfway edible.

''Hmm, for a change the government cooks put out some food that is somewhat fit for consumption,'' the director mumbled.

Geoff agreed for the two of them, by making a polite noise, with Charles. There was not much conversation while they ate, except to remark on the beautiful view that was available from this side of the building. Small talk consisted of how Geoffrey was enjoying his tour of duty as a liaison officer at the embassy for law enforcement agencies; also, they discussed some of the other cases that Ulnar handled when he was with Scotland Yard.

While this was going on, a tall, slim man that was starting to lose his hair came scurrying over to their table. He was the Special Assistant Director of the FBI, Melvin A. Noma, whose main job was to not only oversee the training schools at the FBI Academy at Quantico, Virginia, but to act as a special trouble shooter for Director Dickinson. However, this time he had just recently returned from a trip to the Pearl Harbor Naval Base located in Ouahu. The reason for this particular bit of trouble shooting was to check on an ongoing investigation of a highly placed naval person who was suspected of spying for a far eastern country.

Melvin had just finished dictating his report to his boss when he received a phone call from the Boston Field office. According to the Special Agent in Charge (SAC), the 1st Bank of Boston and the Paul Revere Bank had been robbed at gun point. He also told Melvin that a fax was being sent in the newspaper report of the crime.

Melvin stopped by the Director's right side. Dickinson looked up at him, smiled, and said," Gentlemen, this is my right-hand man, Assistant Director Melvin Noma. Mel, this is Inspector Ulnar Loop formerly of New Scotland Yard and his assistant, Geoffrey Cambridge."

"Gentlemen," he said while shaking their hands. Then, turning to the Director, "Charles, could I have a few minutes of your time?"

""Certainly, please excuse me for a few minutes."

""Of course," said the Inspector.

"The two men walked through the cafeteria, out into the hallway, and then to a conference room that was nearby. There, in privacy, Agent Noma delivered his report from Boston.

"Charles, there's been another two bank robberies up there."

""When did they happen?"

"Day before yesterday. Normally we'd have had a report on it at the end of the month from our field office up there. But the agent in charge, Bill Williams, decided to send it early, along with this small news clipping." He handed the fax of the news clipping over to the FBI Director and continued with his report as Charles studied it. "Bill's been working really close with the Boston P.D. on this.

"So far there have been six of these robberies. Hitting two banks on the same day though, that's a first. And it's the first time that the perps have hit in Boston. All the others have been in the surrounding towns. You know, the small branch banks, the ones that forget to put film in their cameras, or even have the cameras on."

""Did they all go down the same way?"

""No, the others had the people in stocking masks. This one had them in overcoats, hats, and sunglasses. They handed notes to the tellers."

"Then how'd you know they're the same bunch?"

"Andy was going through all the reports at the time and saw that in the other cases the men had accents when speaking English. But, to talk with each other, they'd switch to another. One of the clerks believes that it was Gaelic.

"Why?"

"She's married into an Irish family and heard something that sounded like it once at a family reunion a few years back."

"O.K., then, where's the connection?"

"The same was done at one of the banks this time. Men with what appeared to be Irish accents and spoke in a strange language to each other."

"Anything else?"

""Except for the pump shotguns, and you know a lot of these mutts use those, there's nothing, Charles. But Bill is getting a full report together, including copies of all the police reports and all of his peoples' reports."

""Good. When it comes through, bring it to my office."

""Will do, boss."

"Melvin left the room and returned to his office. Meanwhile, Charles looked down at the faxed copy of the news story from the Boston Globe.

TWO BANKS ROBBED IN BROAD DAYLIGHT

CHAPTER THREE

The next morning as Ulnar had just finished dressing himself, the room phone rang. "Hello?"

"Inspector, this is Geoffrey; I'm down in the lobby, and I'll wait for you by the breakfast bar."

"That's fine Geoff, as soon as I pack, I'll be down."

"Don't worry about that, there's a very fit looking young man near your room. He'll pack for you and make sure that the bags are brought down."

"Is it Harry or George, the two young men that are out of uniform?"

"No. His name is Carey and he's a security person from the Embassy. Harry and George are out on an assignment. In fact, let me radio Carey and let him know that you're ready. He will give two short raps, pause, and then three more short raps."

"Is this drama really necessary?"

"Yes." Geoffrey radioed Carey on a secure frequency and instructed him on the signal. Afterwards, he crossed the large, mostly empty lobby and stood by the left end of the portable breakfast bar. Approximately ten minutes later, Ulnar exited the elevator and looked around the lobby. He spotted Geoff and walked across the vast space to join him.

"Good morning, Geoffrey," he said extending his right hand.

"Good morning, Inspector," Geoff said, taking it. After they shook hands, the two of them entered the dining room side by side. They were seated by a hostess. A few minutes later a waitress appeared and took their orders. When she had left, Ulnar asked about the trip.

"Well Inspector, when we've finished here, we'll go out to the car. Your baggage will have already been loaded. Then it's just a matter of fighting the early morning rush hour traffic. Most of that will disappear once we're outside the beltway."

"Beltway? What on earth is that?"

"When your plane was coming into land, did you notice a larger than life eight lane road encircling the city?"

"Yes, I did. There was a wide ribbon of concrete that appeared to be circular. I've never seen anything so large before."

"Well, that's it, and after that, we should have a fairly easy go of it all the way to Philadelphia, Pennsylvania. That will be our first stop ... we'll get some lunch there."

They both enjoyed a large, healthy breakfast. Geoff and Ulnar talked through it, with Ulnar asking Mr. Cambridge about himself. After they ate, they paid the bill, leaving a tip, and left the dining room.

They walked out into the lobby which was starting to fill with people who were checking out of the hotel. They found a sarge sofa, sat down, and continued their chat. There was no sign of hotel security. Geoffrey was telling Ulnar about his home life and what made him decide on a career with Scotland Yard, when they were interrupted.

Someone had called out Geoffrey's name. He turned his head towards the elevators and saw the man from Embassy Security. Carey Cause worthy was standing to one side of the elevators with the Inspector's luggage. The two men walked over to him.

"Sir," he said to Mr. Cambridge, "I have all of his luggage, and I've just radioed the car. Special Agent Adams has just pulled up to the curb and is waiting."

The three of them turned and walked out of the hotel. The sky was partially cloudy with the air already turning humid. They crossed the sidewalk to the car; Geoff opened the rear door for Ulnar, who got in. Then he turned to Carey and helped him load the Inspector's baggage into the already open trunk. He double checked with Carey to be certain that the hotel bill had been taken care of and got into the front passenger seat of the vehicle.

The two men greeted Samantha who returned their greetings as she pulled into the morning traffic; the car was immediately swallowed up in the late rush hour crunch of cars. They drove through town and crossed the Anacostia River. From there they headed out to 1-495, the beltway. They drove past Boling Air Force Base and a few minutes later, the sewage treatment plant. They got on the Beltway on the Maryland side of D.C. Once they came to 1-95 and started driving north, the traffic thinned out, and their driving became much easier.

As they drove towards Baltimore, Special Agent Adams asked the Inspector what had made him stay in the Science of Fingerprints for so many years.

"I believe that it was a sense of accomplishment... doing something that was needed ... a challenge, if you will. No matter how far I went in science, there was always a challenge. Every part of what I did helped someone ... even the grim side of the profession."

"What was the grim side; I didn't think there was one."

"Oh, there is," Ulnar continued. "It's the printing of the palms and fingers of people who have died one way or another, but there is no identification on them. Of course, there's a great deal of satisfaction when, through taking a good set of inked prints, the person is identified and his or her loved ones can be told. Lockerbie, Scotland is a good example."

"Oh, where the airliner was blown up by terrorists and the plane literally fell out of the sky and onto the town killing even more people."

"Exactly. It was very grim work, but this way, people knew. They didn't have to wonder anymore," he finished as he looked out the window at the passing scenery. Ulnar continued looking out the window for a good while, taking in the vast acres of woods, farmland, and the new housing developments that were springing up all over, it seemed. The silence from the back seat of the rented vehicle grew as Ulnar stared outwards at nothing in particular while his mind went backwards into the past, remembering all of those bodies that he had printed for identification and then comparing them for elimination purposes against latent impressions. No, he thought, it wasn't the prettiest part of the profession, nor the easiest. But it was very necessary.

It was necessary for those people that had drowned, that had been burned, that had been dead for a few days before being found. Of course, there were problems that went with this part of the profession. One problem was how to get those fingerprints and those palmprints.

The skin may be decomposing, or it is too hard because of mummification. Or even trying to find those small pieces of skin that have not been burned. Using all of your knowledge and reading articles written by other experts dealing with those subjects, while attempting to find a solution to each of those problems. To find enough ridge detail so that a positive identification can be made. Yes, it was very necessary to the victims.

It was also necessary for the victims' families. Who was going to speak to them for the victim. To say, "Yes, this is me. This is who I was while I was alive." It was grim work, alright, he thought to himself. But some of the best identifications that I made came from finding out who some unknown deceased was. And then telling their loved ones. All because of two facts. There are no two fingers, palm, or footprints exactly the same.

After some time had passed, no one really knew how long, and Samantha and Geoffrey quietly talked up front, Ulnar broke the silence. "I suppose the greatest thing about my field is that there are no two prints exactly the same."

"I've heard that statement many times while working at the Bureau," Samantha said.

''Believe me, it's quite true. With almost fifty years of working in science, I have never personally seen, read, or heard of two different fingers being identical. Not even in identical twins. That's why we say that this science is the Only Positive Means of Identification. When I make an identification, it is based on the principle that I have already mentioned plus one more, and that is because those same fingerprints remain the same throughout a person's life. My training, knowledge, and experience tell me that this fingerprint over here is identical with that one over there. And that is a very good feeling. However, there are many times that trying to find that identification is a very long process.'' Smiling to himself he thought that yes, it was a very good feeling. One that he was beginning to realize that he missed more than he thought was possible.

"Have you ever taught or talked to children in schools about fingerprints or about what you do?"

Geoffrey spoke up, "Yes, I should say he does ... or rather did, before his retirement. I was in one of his classes at the Yard ten years ago."

"I used to teach all of the new fingerprint and crime scene people, but I never spoke at any schools. I really don't know if anyone did."

They were coming to Baltimore and Agent Adams needed all of her concentration focused on her driving because of the traffic. The Inspector and Geoffrey watched the buildings go by as they drove through the city; they also noticed that the weather had completely cleared. Finally, they left the city with its large harbor area and entered the fields, woods, and urban sprawl of the country. It was a peaceful ride; in fact, it was so peaceful with the warmth of the sun entering the car and the hum of the tires on the road, that Ulnar dozed off. It was such a nice drive that it took Mr. Cambridge until they were about an hour outside of Philadelphia to realize that Ulnar Loop was no longer in the land of the awake and the alert.

He turned to Samantha and quietly asked her whether or not she could get an update on the robberies in the Boston area. She said that while they stopped for lunch in the City of Brotherly Love, she would go to the local FBI Field Office and make the necessary phone calls. Then she would rejoin the two men for a short tour of the Independence National Historical Park. She would fill them in on the status at that time.

"When you get back," he said, "I'll make an excuse to slip away and make a check with the Yard's liaison office at the Embassy and see if there is any news from Harry and George on the other investigation. I somehow believe that something may happen to him," he pointed back to Ulnar who was still sound asleep, his head tilted over and resting on his right shoulder. "Long before we find out who is needing so much of your currency."

They drove on in silence to Philadelphia, with Geoffrey enjoying the country scenery and watching the towns and cities slip silently by in a steady stream. Samantha drove and watched her rearview mirror for anyone who might be following them. As they entered the city limits, Ulnar woke up with an embarrassed start.

"Oh! I daresay ... please excuse my rudeness...I...I didn't...! did not expect to do that... sleep, I mean."

Geoffrey spoke up, 'Don't worry about its Inspector. It happens on long drives in nice weather. But you did wake up in time for our lunch stop; what would you like to eat?"

"It doesn't make much difference as long as it is not government cooking."

Samantha laughed at that and promised him that that would not happen. She suggested an outdoor eatery that she knew about. It was not too far from the historical park. The two men agreed that lunch sounded like a fine idea and eating outside, even better. The three of them exited 1-95 at Market Street and drove west towards downtown.

They drove past the Liberty Bell Pavilion, through Independence Mall, and continued on for another three blocks, turning right onto eighth street towards the Gallery Mall. Across the street from the mall was a small outdoor dining area. After parking the car, they walked back to the sidewalk cafe. The sun was out and still not a cloud in the sky. There was a very light breeze blowing from the northwest, and because of a storm front that had passed through the other day, the temperature was in the mid-seventies according to the weatherman. They found a place to sit and waited for someone to take their order. The three agreed, the weather couldn't be more perfect.

"This is very much like the weather back at Twinned Loop when I left on this journey." After a hesitation, "I've seen many a wonderful and beautiful sight back in the British Isles, but I really never expected to see much of the same sights here, in the states. I thought that it would be all smokestacks and factories with terrible lung crushing smog."

"Many cities are like that, and even this city can be miserable when the heat and humidity rise. You're right though, there are some wonderful places in this country." Sam said while she idly twiddled her fork.

"Geoffrey, what made you join Scotland Yard?" She asked, changing the subject.

"I'm not sure if I joined it or, it, chose m ... "

"Ya wanna order?" The waiter asked, rudely interrupting their conversation.

"Excuse me?" Sam asked the waiter, staring at him in disbelief.

"I asked if you wanna order, lady."

"Since you put your request in such a fine, friendly, fashion, then yes, I believe that we will, thank you." The three of them placed their orders. After the waiter had turned and walked back into the cafe, Sam said, "Such nice friendly people they have serving the public."

"Yes, his parents must be very proud of him. And with such a command of the English language, he must be attending University." The Inspector added.

Thirty minutes passed by and then the object of their insincere worship returned with the meals. He placed them on the table, not bothering to ask who got what, in an incorrect order. He stood there watching them, not saying a word. Finally, Geoffrey Cambridge looked up, first at, and then into, the gloomy, glassy eyes of the young man and noticed why he did not appear to care.

"Is there something else, young man?" He asked. The waiter suddenly turned and walked away. "I cannot understand why anyone would use that garbage, especially when they are working. I'm sorry, but I have seen enough of that...that... stuff... destroy good, healthy, lives. Perhaps one day, someone will care enough to tell him that he is a fool and does not really need it." He added, almost to himself.

"Why Geoffrey, I would never have expected such a statement from you; considering that you are with the Anti-Terrorist Branch at the Yard." Ulnar said in surprise.

"Sir, this problem, as some people call it, touches almost everyone's life ... some more than others. Some in a more personal way," he added very quietly. "But I forgot, you worked in the science area of crime, not the streets. Even terrorists were not immune to it. And even some of the wonderful people that I have worked with have had their children damaged from it. It is an epidemic and like an epidemic it should be stamped out by almost any means. We can't tramp on the liberties that have been built up over the last few centuries to kill this nastiness; they may never be regained. However, there is a lot that we can do that is not being done." He stopped suddenly. Sheepishly, he added, "Sorry, didn't mean to get up on my soapbox."

Feeling stung by the reference about his laboratory work, Ulnar started "Geoffrey .... ," and trailed off. The man was right, and he knew it. Furthermore, he started to feel ashamed of his retirement. He should not have cut himself off from the world the way he did, there was so much he could have given instead. After all he thought, I may be seventy, but I am certainly no old fogy, ready to order my tombstone and coffin. The look on his face became harder, sterner. George, I will change that.

It was as if Geoff and Sam could read his thoughts. They saw the look on his face and knew that the Inspector was once again walking among the true living. Not wanting to give this away to him, Samantha changed the subject. "By the way Geoff I saw your official record; the Embassy was kind enough to pass it along to us, although it does appear that some of the files were altered because of a need to know. It was still impressive."

"Thank you. Of course, you realize that it was a mutual thing. I was allowed a glance of yours as well. Also, very impressive."

The Inspector remained silent while the three of them ate their meals. Samantha finished hers and excused herself. "I'm going over to the local field office and check to see if there have been any more robberies." She got up, left the table, and walked through the rest of the tables to the entrance of the cafe. Then she continued on briskly for three blocks to the Federal Building.

Once she was there and had taken the elevator up to the right floor, she showed her ID to the guard and was admitted into the Philadelphia FBI Field Office. Special Agent Samantha Adams reported to the Agent in Charge, who was expecting her. He left his office while she made a secure phone call to Special Assistant Director Melvin Noma who came on the line after one ring.

"Right on time, Samantha," he said. "So far there have been no other bank robberies in the Boston area. However, if they keep to their timetable, the robbers should hit by ten AM. tomorrow morning at the latest. Oh, by the way, how is your guest doing?"

"He's doing fine, sir. I believe that he has finally come out of the shell that I was told about... there might be an important change happening."

"That's good to hear. I'll pass that along to Director Dickinson. Anything else?"

"Only that we will be going on the tour of the historical park; it's still on. Of course, with forty buildings in it, we won't be able to see everything. Maybe it will give him another view of America; one that he may not have fully comprehended. Anyhow, we'll see."

"Then enjoy your tour. And check in tomorrow morning before you leave for Boston." He reminded her. They said their goodbyes, she hung up the phone, and motioned the Special Agent in Charge to return to his office.

When he arrived and had shut the door, Sam told him about a car that had seemed to have followed them from just after they had left the interstate to their turn onto Ninth Street. "It appeared strange," she finished.

"What kind of vehicle was it?" he asked.

"A 93 or 94 Mercury Sable, or maybe a Ford Taurus. They look so much alike ... mmm, red in color."

"What made it come to your attention?"

"We had just passed Front Street and about two cars back this vehicle, that I described to you, pulled out in front of a large construction truck. I just happened to look at the rearview mirror to see if anyone had pulled off at the same time behind us ... and if so, who. I saw the car pull out from a parking spot. Whoever it was, acted like he was in a real hurry. Then he slowed down and kept pace with the rest of the traffic. When I turned onto Ninth, that same car slowed down and quickly pulled over to the side of the street and double parked. When I walked over here, there was no sign of it."

"I'll check with the local police and see if there have been any cars of the type you described that have been stolen. Of course, if it had happened today, then most likely it wouldn't be in their computers. Call back here in about an hour or so; meantime, enjoy your tour." She told him that she would and left the office.

On the way back she decided to take a little detour and see if anyone was following. There didn't appear to be, so she went back to the outdoor cafe. The two men were standing at the entrance of it waiting for her. "Is there anything new?" Mr. Cambridge asked.

"No, but I'm to check back in the morning before we finish our trip to Boston." She did not want to say anything about the car in front of Ulnar. She would wait until later to tell Geoff the three of them walked back to the car and drove back to the park area. After finding a parking spot they walked towards Independence Hall, which is located on Chestnut Street. Just before they got to it, Geoff asked a park ranger where there might be a men's room.

After being told, he walked in that direction. On the way he saw what he wanted, a telephone booth. He called the Embassy, and the Yard liaison operative answered the phone.

"Liaison Office, Barnes speaking, may I help you?"

"Michael, this is Geoff; is there any news on the leak from Commander Cummings?"

"It's only been a day and he is trying to keep it low key. So that if the leak started from there, the party responsible will not be alarmed. However, there has been a short message from Harry and George. It seems that they drove into the central part of Boston to meet with their informant and…."

"And what?"

"And she was found by the police in the inner harbor."

"How did they find out; I know they didn't call the locals."

"No, it was one of my people on the force. I told him that there was a contact that didn't show up at the appointed time and place. He asked me for a description and after I was finished, he said that he would call right back. Sure enough, five minutes later he rang back and told me about the Jane Doe they found in the harbor. Been there about a day according to the Medical Examiner."

"Well, that's a fine kettle of fish. Hopefully, something will break on the other end. What are George and Harry going to do now?"

"They said they were going to keep a low profile in case she talked before she was dropped into the harbor and wait for word from either the Yard or you."

"Thanks, Michael. I'll be in touch after we get to Boston."

"Good hunting, Geoff." They ran off, and he walked back to Samantha and Ulnar.

"Thought you'd fallen in, Agent Adams and I were about to call in the marines." This brought about a good laugh as they entered Independence Hall. The tour guide explained that the hall was begun in 1732 and was finished in 1748 or so. He went on to say that the Liberty Bell hung in the steeple until 1781. At that time the steeple was removed because of decay and the bell was hung in a back hall on the first floor. In 1976 it was moved to Liberty Bell Pavilion which was built for the Bicentennial. Among some of the antiques that they saw was the Sun Chair that George Washington sat in, and the inkstand that was used for the Declaration of Independence and the Constitution of the United States.

Ulnar was very impressed. "The history in this building is overwhelming. I never had any idea that it was so ... so .. "

''Impressive?" Agent Adams asked.

"Yes," he replied reverently, softly.

"The history of this young country is, to say the least, colorful." Geoffrey added. ''No disrespect intended, Samantha. But from the colonization of your original thirteen colonies to the Louisiana Purchase from France. Then there was Texas and the Texans' revolt against Mexico. Then you obtained California. And your Alaskan and Hawaiian Territories. Then, there is all of history in between."

"Yes, it may be young, but we have built a lot of history in that short time. In a way though, it's too bad that the children of this country don't take a more active interest in it. There is so much, that, well ... how could they become bored?"

''Mayhaps if their parents became more interested, they would."

''Yes, and perhaps some of them would find a love of it and become teachers; then they would pass that love onto another, and another, so that it would not die." That caused a pause in the conversation, and they left the hall. They walked out into the bright sunshine of a clear and free day. The light breeze was still blowing as they continued over to a crosswalk in the middle of the block. When they reached it, Geoff and Sam stopped to watch the crowds around them, and she passed on the information about the car that had followed them. Ulnar was not paying much attention to them and after looking right and then left, he stepped off the curb and onto the crosswalk.

Suddenly, there was a squeal of smoking tires and the high-pitched revving of an engine. Ulnar looked to his left to see a car come screaming towards him. He stood rooted to the spot like a deer caught in someone's headlights. When it appeared that he was about to get hit, two pairs of hands grabbed him and yanked him back onto the sidewalk. The three of them landed in a tangled heap of bodies, having knocked down a number of people that were immediately behind them. Samantha struggled to release herself from the pile, finally getting to her feet and looking down the street at the weaving, speeding vehicle. All she could see was a possible type and color; it was too far away to see the tag. Then the car took a hard right on two screeching wheels and raced south on Fourth Street.

She went back to the Inspector and Geoffrey who were just now getting to their feet. He looked at her and she very slightly shook her head. Others were also getting up and she went over to help them. "Is everyone all right," she asked, just as a policeman came running down the sidewalk. He slowed down and walked over to the crowd of people checking themselves. "Is everybody okay?"

People nodded and said that there were only a few scrapes and scratches. No one needed any medical attention. The officer then asked, "Did anyone see what happened?"

The other people told him that they did not see what happened. Samantha said that her friends, she pointed to the two men, ... ''Were just starting to cross the street when the car came out of nowhere; it looked like a drunk driver who might have run a red light up the block." No, she did not get a good look at the vehicle. He took down what little information she gave him and radioed his precinct. He relayed his small amount of information to them and asked that some paramedics come to the scene and check out the people. When that was done, he told the tourists to wait for the medics and told the crowd that had gathered to go about their business.

He walked over to Samantha and asked her to sign a report down at the precinct. She showed him her identification. "That might be somewhat difficult, officer. These two gentlemen standing here beside me are official guests in this country. It would be appreciated if their names be kept out of this. I hope that you understand, Officer ... "

"Gronsky, ma'am."

"Yes, Officer Gransky. I hope that you understand that it would be an embarrassment to this country if it were to be known that an official guest to this country who is a personal friend of the Queen of England were to be hauled down to your precinct and grilled about a possible hit and run involving a drunk that normally would not take more than five minutes of your time." She took him off to one side and said, "Besides, sir, we can't even tell you, his name. I will get in touch with the Agent in Charge of the local field office. He will get in touch with your superiors and tell them what they need to know."

"All right, it looks like I don't have any real choice in the matter. Go on about your business as soon as the paramedics get done with you."

They had already arrived and were checking everyone over for any possible serious injuries that might not be apparent to the victims. Finally, they got too Ulnar and after a thorough check, declared him to have a clean bill of health. The three of them crossed the street with no more interference from_ traffic. Ulnar told them that he was foolish not to have remembered to look first left, then right; what with this being such a backward country.

Meanwhile, several blocks away. "Saints preserved the lucky sod. We missed."

"I could have sworn that we had the old goat. He was dead where he stood. And did you get a good look at that dark haired lass that helped pull him back to safety?" asked the leader.

''No. Do you think that she was the one that we saw earlier, driving their so-called safe car?"

"Could be. One thing's for certain, the lads in Boston are not going to be happy: what with him getting away like that. And" he continued, holding up his scarred left hand to stop any interruption, "They will be even less pleased to know that there might be another guard with him."

"Where do we go now?"

"To the yanks' Big Apple," replied the leader. "That's their next stop. We'll follow them and wait for the right moment while they go touring around the city." They left the recently stolen car where it was and caught a bus to the other side of the city. There, in a shopping mall parking lot, they got their own rented vehicle and traveled to New York City.

The three subjects of this discussion were now at the Liberty Bell Pavilion. After that they walked up the Independence Mall where they saw the U.S. Mint, the Free Quaker Meeting House, Betsy Ross's House, and many other historical attractions that are in this area of the Independence National Historical Park. Samantha told them that she wished they had more time to visit some of these buildings, but they had a schedule to keep. Ulnar made a mental note to come back and visit this sight when his official duties were finished.

An hour later they were well on their way to New York City. The three of them continued up I-95 past Edison, New Jersey. Just past Newark, they got onto the Pulaski Skyway and went East; then they entered the Holland Tunnel. On the other side of the tunnel, they were in Manhattan and turned left onto the Avenue of the Americas. This led them to Central Park South. A left, a quick right, and they were on the West side of Central Park. Finally, they were in downtown Manhattan. The three of them found a nice hotel not far from the Lincoln Center.

They checked in and got two adjoining rooms on the fifth floor. After Samantha had unpacked her suitcases, she called the Philadelphia field office to see if anything had come up in the local computer on the possible stolen car. The Special Agent in Charge said that there was nothing yet.

"Tell them to look south of Chestnut Street, probably somewhere near Fourth Street. They were in a hurry and with the park police all around the area, they might have spooked and gotten rid of it quicker than normal."

"Why that particular area?" Oh, wait a minute. You're not going to tell me that the possible drunk driver that almost hit some visitors in the park area was you and your charges. I don't envy you your next call. You know how they feel about a breach in procedure."

"Yes, to the question, and yes to the statement about procedure. However, it was a judgement call at the time, and I didn't want the Inspector to get the idea that he was almost killed on purpose. I had to get control of the situation quickly and the way I handled it seemed to be the best way at the time. Oh, and you will call the local precinct and let them know what happened ... at least to a certain extent."

The Agent in Charge was rapidly writing all of this information down in his own shorthand. Finally, "Got it. Is there anything else that I should know?"

"Nothing. Let me know what you find out on that car, and thanks."

Her next call was not going to be pleasant; however, she did not get where she was by being overly cautious. Granted, sticking your neck out was not the best way to climb the ladder of success at the Bureau, but neither was waiting for someone else to make a decision. So, she had no doubt about what she would say.

After several rings the phone on the other end was picked up. "Hello?"

"Good evening, sir. I have some bad news. It seems that our bait worked; the Inspector was almost run down this afternoon. I'm afraid that I did not get a good look at the car because Mr. Cambridge and I were too busy pulling him to safety. Besides, it's quite likely that the car was stolen. These people are not stupid."

"Have you reported this to the field office?"

"Yes, I have, and the SAC said that he would get right on it."

"That's good, but I don't especially care for the way that we're handling this situation. It seems to be a little too dangerous for our subject.

"I understand that sir. However, it was the idea of Scotland Yard to do it this way. Ifwe are going to help, sir, then we should follow their plan. They have a pretty good track record for this sort of operation."

"Hmmm. Yes, I see what you mean. Okay, what's your next move?"

"I'm not entirely sure yet, sir. I still believe the best way to handle this is to just act naturally and go on with the sightseeing as planned. All we can do is be as ready as possible."

"You're quite right. Again, good luck and please try very hard not to lose the Inspector; I don't think that the British will find it very amusing if we lose him."

"Thank you, sir." She hung up the phone and then picked it back up, so that she could call Geoff's room.

"Can you talk? Good. I've finished my call with Washington, and everything is still on for tomorrow. No, I don't think that there is any other way of handling it. Uh huh…. Uh huh…. Right…. I agree completely. We'll take the subway, and with any luck we may get one of them. With it not being rush hour we may be able to spot them before anything can happen." She sighed and said, "At least I hope that it will come out that way. Oh? Of course, I'll be right over. Unlock the door between the rooms."

She heard the other door unlock just as she did the same to her' s; she opened both doors and entered the other room. In the background she could hear the shower running.

"The Inspector decided to freshen up a bit before supper. He said that he was feeling a little grimy from this afternoon's excitement.

Listen, I need you to stay here with him while I quickly run over to our U.N. Consulate and ring up Commander Cummings. I know that just three days have passed since this started, but I'm hoping they might at least have a small lead on the leak. Things are moving fast, and we can't afford to be too far behind.

"That's not a problem. I'll leave these two doors open so that if my phone rings I'll be able to answer it."

He looked at her strangely and asked, 'Why don't you just call the switchboard and have them transfer your calls to this phone?"

''I would but remember that we registered separately. We don't want to make it too easy for them to find out for sure that there are two of us here in the hotel guarding him. Same with tomorrow; I'll stand back out of the way, as much as possible, that is."

He hit his head with his right hand and said, "Good grief, am I getting a case of the stupid, or what. I didn't even think of that."

"That's all right, we all forget something, sometime."

''Yes, but in my case, it could be fatal, and I'm not being paid to get terminally dumb."

''Fine, we'll discuss this later; right now, you'd better get going before it gets too late."

Geoffrey Cambridge left the room and took the back stairs. On reaching the lobby level, he went down a back hallway and through the kitchen. He left the hotel through the loading dock and went out the alley to the street behind the hotel. He hailed a cab and took it three blocks in the opposite direction that he wanted to go. He recklessly ran down the up escalator, almost out of control, of the subway. At the bottom, he looked back to see if anyone was trying to follow him. Then he briskly walked through the turnstile and jumped on a train that was just about to leave.

He rode it for five stops, then he got off at the last minute, ran to the other side of the platform and got on a train going in another direction. This, he rode for about an hour so that he could check on anyone that might have made it with him. Seeing no one, he got off the train. Taking his time, he went up to the street level and hailed another cab.

He took this cab to within three blocks of the consulate. On a pay phone, he called the office of the Cultural Attache introducing himself by code. They asked where he was, and he told them. "Wait there." The voice on the other end said and hung up.

Fifteen minutes later a rental car came, picked him up, and took him to the British Consulate. He went down to the basement to the secure communications room and called up the yard.

''New Scotland Yard, Wesley Speaking.''

"This is Cambridge, put me through to Commander Cummings; he's expecting this call."

"Cummings here, good evening, Geoffrey."

"Good evening, sir. I have news, both good and bad, I'm afraid. The good news is that the felons took the bait today and tried to do away with the Inspector."

''How?''

''Ulnar was almost run down this afternoon in the City of Brotherly Love. They tried to make it look like a drunk driver, but since we already knew that we were followed into the city ... well," Geoffrey let the statement trail off.

"Yes, I see what you mean. Were you able to get a look at them, or the plate from the vehicle?"

"That's the bad news, sir. No, we didn't; we had our hands full pulling the Inspector back, out of the way. Besides, the car will most likely show up as being stolen. These people are not stupid. Anything on your end, Commander?"

"Some good news for us. In the past three days we've been quite busy. We've had the living styles, acquaintances, and history of everyone who has had any knowledge of the Inspector's movements, and prior dealings with his trip, carefully studied and updated. I can tell you that it was quite a chore, and we had to let the Intelligence Services do the work so that there would be no suspicions aroused. They've worked very hard and have been able to narrow the list of suspects down to just three of the staff and that brings up another point.

Since there are people who have not been cleared, and two of them are in very sensitive positions, you will not call her until further notice. Instead, you will receive and pass any messages concerning this subject through Ambassador Ambrose at our Embassy in Washington. He will be your only contact with us until we find the traitor." There was silence, and then the Commander spoke once more.

"One more thing Geoffrey. Call George Black before you leave the Consulate; he has some urgent information for the three of you. Have a safe journey." He hung up.

Geoffrey's next call went to the Churned-Up Inn, in Buttermilk. After five rings, he spoke to George.

"They hit," George said with a muffled voice, "Just before the bank closed. Excuse me, I have a partial mouthful of fish and chips. Of course, it is not the same full-bodied version that is to be found back in jolly old England."

"I'm glad that you're enjoying such a fine nourishing meal, George, but please help an old beat-up investigator by enlightening him with the name of the bank."

"Oh, sorry, sir. It was a small branch of the Paul Revere Bank that is located in a small city north of here. Just a moment. Ah ... here it is. The name of the place is Smaller Wormwood. Anyhow," he said while swallowing another mouthful of food, "For the first time they got careless. They shot a bank guard; he's in stable condition at a local medical center. At the other banks you may remember, the robbers went out of their way to avoid shooting anyone. This time they were caught off guard by the security. Apparently, the guards had decided not to take any chances after the other robberies in the area. Then, while the bad guys were distracted, someone set off the alarm. They left before they could get any money.

"How did they know that it was the same gang?"

"Same clothing; I guess they think that the long overcoats, hats, and sunglasses make them look like gangsters. They like that look of being bad."

"Okay, good report, George. I'll check in tomorrow morning with the Ambassador before we leave for Boston. If nothing else has happened by the time we get there, we'll go on to Smaller Wormwood and see if we can get any leads. By the by, where do you want to meet?"

"We'll meet at the Boston Police Commissioner's Office. I'll make contact with the Ambassador tonight and have it arranged. That way if anything new can be added, we'll all be updated at the same time. Don't forget to give this information to your new partners."

"Right. And let me know if you turn up any information on the people that are after the Inspector. We can't forget that it's still part of our assignment. Enjoy your meal." He rang off. Before he left the building he was stopped by security and picked up a small electronic device. An hour and a half later, he was back in his room.

When he walked in, the Inspector said, 'There you are my boy. Samantha's in the next room. Oh, and I've been watching the most marvelous show on horticulture."

Geoffrey walked into the other room after knocking on the adjoining door. "I'm through with my errand. And I have some new information for both of you. Well, at least part of it is for you both. The other, I'll have to tell you later, Samantha."

"That will be fine." They walked back into Geoffrey's room and got the Inspector.

The three of them left the room after taking some precautions and went down to the dining room which boasted an excellent menu. While they ate, Geoffrey filled them both in on the newest bank heist.

"There's not much anyone can do without them leaving something behind, or having their hats or sunglasses magically disappear so that we can see their faces," the Inspector said. After a moment of silence he asked, 'Has there been any mention of them wearing gloves? I don't recall anyone mentioning it."

"You're right!" Sam exclaimed. That's something we'd better check on tomorrow. But they've also been very careful not to touch anything, or at least there's been no talk of it." They finished dinner and went back to their rooms.

The next morning, they got together for breakfast in the dining room. "Well Ulnar, what would you like to see first?" Sam hesitated, then added, "If I remember correctly, you only wanted three attractions. The Empire State Building, the United Nations, and the Statue of Liberty." She ticked these items off on her fingers as she named them.

"Are they near each other?"

"Not really, but in this city it's not a problem. We can take a subway to all but the statue ... why I asked though, was to make a suggestion. Since it's a nice morning and the humidity is supposed to rise later, why don't the two of you catch a cab over to Central Park and take a horse-drawn cab ride around the park. I have some things to do; so, I'll meet you in an hour or so on the 102nd floor observatory at the Empire State Building."

"That sounds like an excellent suggestion," Geoffrey said. Inspector, I think it would be a wonderful way to let our breakfasts digest; in comfort and peace."

They entered the park at the 61st Street entrance and hired the first horse drawn carriage that they saw. Samantha was right; it was a beautiful morning. The sun was out casting early morning shadows through the trees. The birds were out singing and looking for food along with all of the squirrels. As they wound their way around the park on a well-kept black top road, Ulnar watched the Americans at play. Or at least he thought of it that way. They were out in droves; riding bicycles, jogging, walking, their bodies running with sweat, all of them with their own personal bottle of water; such a strange sight. To himself he said, these overly health-conscious nuts had better be careful with all of these squirrels around.

They went past small ponds and lakes. They saw the Belvedere Castle; they went past the Metropolitan Museum of Art; and at the end of their ride, they saw the Central Park Zoo. For Ulnar and Geoff, this little ride had been a pleasant diversion from their trip. But of course, more was to come with the three sights that Ulnar wanted to see. So, at the end of the ride they hailed a taxi and took it to the Empire State Building.

Upon entering the building, they waited in line with the rest of the tourists for the express elevator. They found it interesting watching the floors of the building go by. First every floor and then every tenth floor until, in a matter of minutes, they came to the top. They exited the elevator and took an escalator the rest of the way up.

Samantha was already there. In fact, she had been there for almost an hour. She was watching the people, trying to see if anyone looked overly suspicious. So far, nothing. Then she spotted Geoff and Ulnar and saw a pair of eyes following them closely. The pair of eyes belonged to one of the two casually dressed men at one of the binoculars. One was looking at the surrounding city through them; the other was pretending to read a tourist map. But his eyes were watching over the top of it instead. Sam shook her head very slightly from side to side, letting Geoffrey know not to approach her. Ulnar was too engrossed in the view to notice her off to the farthest corner. She pretended to watch the ant sized traffic and people down below, while really keeping an eye on the two new subjects. They were trying so hard to look normal, to fit in, that they really stuck out like sore thumbs.

After taking in the vast view from all sides of the observatory, Ulnar and Geoffrey left. They stopped briefly at the gift shops to see what kind of tourist type nick knacks were on display. Their two shadows followed at a safe distance. After a few minutes Agent Adams left the observation deck and headed directly for the nearest subway station and took up a post there. Meanwhile the Inspector and Mr. Cambridge took their time leaving the building and heading for the same station. The two strangers continued to follow.

Everyone took the subway to the U.N. Building. Samantha rode in the next car still keeping an eye on the followers. At the United Nations, Geoff already had tickets for a tour and the two of them went inside. The strangers did not; they stayed outside and waited. So did she.

''What do you think he's up too?''

"I told you before, he's taking a busman's holiday. Don't worry, he doesn't suspect a thing." The leader said. "They'll be out in a wee bit and when the opportunity arises, we'll take our shot. The British think they're so clever; his bodyguard won't expect a thing until it's all over."

''Have you seen the dark-haired lass?''

''No. And I don't think we will. She was just a good Samaritan who tried to save a life.''

CHAPTER FOUR

About an hour and a half later, Geoff and his charge walked out of the UN. and started towards the nearest subway station. Sam followed the followers. They went down, deep into the bowels of the station to catch their train. Sam stood. A few feet away from the two strangers. Geoffrey and the Inspector were standing behind the wide yellow line beside the tracks. A small crowd had gathered to catch the same train. One of the shadowers suddenly rushed forward with his arms stretched out in front of him, his hands open, just as the train started to enter the station. He pushed hard against the back of a woman who was directly behind Ulnar. She cried out in surprise, her arms spinning in the air trying to catch her balance.

But it was too late. She went into him. Hard. He in turn stumbled over the line and lost his balance; he fell to the tracks right in front of the slowing train. There were screams, confusion. People pushed forward to try and see what had happened. Perhaps to get a view of the gory remains of the poor person who fell onto the tracks while trying to become a hood ornament for the train. The man who did the pushing made a mistake by hesitating for just a second or two, to see the results of his push. The other, the one with the scarred hand, took off at a rapid rate for the stairs.

Samantha came up behind the killer, and in the confusion, took him down. She had him cuffed and was holding him before he knew what had happened. She yelled for help. A Transit Policeman came up to her and she held up her identification. "Hold this man for me. He just pushed an important visitor to this country in front of that train," she said, pointing towards the tracks. "We have to get it backed up so that we can recover the body."

"I've already called dispatch and the train should be backing up soon."

Just as he spoke those words the train did exactly that. When it was back far enough, Geoff jumped down onto the tracks trying frantically to see the remains of a body. Then he looked under the overhang of the platform. There was Ulnar, bent over, slowly attempting to pull himself out. "Help me Geoffrey," he said, holding out his left hand. Mr. Cambridge grabbed it and helped him out from under the overhang. He pushed the Inspector from behind while Samantha and some of the other passengers grabbed his arms and pulled. He cried out in pain when they grabbed his right arm. After a short struggle, he was standing on the platform; although, he was a little unsteady on his feet. Geoffrey pulled himself up, and with Sam's help, they steadied the Inspector. The three of them walked over to a nearby bench and sat Ulnar down.

While Geoff was checking Ulnar over for any injuries Agent Adams went over to her prisoner. The Transit Officer now had reinforcements, and they were getting the crowd under control. The train moved forward again, and the people started boarding.

She asked the Sergeant in charge to radio in and get some help from the New York Field Office. "But please stay here for the time being." A look of concern crossed her face as she looked over her shoulder at Ulnar. "Will he be okay?" She asked Goeffrey.

"Should be, the worst of it appears to be a broken right arm. The rest are just some scrapes and small cuts. We should take him to a hospital for treatment."

"We'll take care of that as soon as my back up appears. What about the woman that was pushed into him; is she all right?"

A nearby Transit Officer pointed to his left at an older woman being helped by officers. "She is a little shaken. We've called for paramedics ... they should be here soon."

Much of the crowd had by now either left the station or were on the train. Just the police, victims, and an angry suspect were left. A few minutes later Sam Adam's backup came and so did the paramedics. One of them went over to the woman to check her out. The other came over to where Ulnar sat. He looked at the arm and immediately went to his case and got a splint which he put on the arm so that no more damage could be done.

The agents from the New York Field Office took charge of the sullen suspect. The Inspector was an official foreign guest of this country, so the FBI would handle the case. All of the officers were cautioned to keep silent on the situation, although it was known that some would talk, and to come by the field office to get their statements taken. The agents led their passive prisoner out of the subway station and to a car. Thirty minutes later they were at the Federal Building and questioning him. Ulnar and the woman were put on stretchers and taken by ambulance to the nearby hospital.

Samantha and Geoffrey went with him, along with a detail of five agents for security. When the Inspector saw the fuss being made at the emergency room to get him some help, he firmly put his foot down. "I refuse to be treated differently. I will await my tum just as these others must."

The two security officers knew that there would be no changing his mind on this just as they knew he was going to be asking some very pointed and direct questions after he was treated. While Geoff and Sam waited, they saw the older woman, the innocent pawn in this madness, being wheeled into one of the treatment cubicles. "Is that her," Ulnar asked as she passed by.

Geoffrey slowly nodded his head. Ulnar got up and, holding his injured arm, went to the cubicle that she was in. "Dear lady, are you going to be all right? I'm dreadfully sorry that you were caught up in this mess. Oh, by the way, my name is Ulnar Loop," he said and did a formal bow as he introduced himself.

I'm Arlene Arbuckle and thank you for your concern. But I think I'm going to be fine; at least the paramedics believe so. Except, that is, for these scrapes and the stiffness from my fall. The people with you, though, wanted me to be brought here for observation. You know," she gestured with her hand, "To make sure there are no hidden problems. I'm just a little bruised up and embarrassed." She sighed, "But I don't really like it here," she said, first looking up at the fluorescent fixture in the ceiling, then down at the stark, highly waxed white floor tiles. The whole tiny, curtained area looked so cold and sterile. She shivered.

"Are you cold madam?"

"No, it...it's just...," her voice trailed off. She turned her face away from the Inspector; he could hear her weeping.

"Who were you going to see?" He asked softly, gently.

"I was on my way to see my daughter and my new grandson. I live in Brooklyn, and I was changing trains when I was pushed. I'm so very sorry that you got hurt."

"Mrs. Arbuckle, you should not worry about that. I'll heal." He reached down with his good left hand and gently touched her shoulder. Then he turned away and went back to his curtained area.

"Geoffrey Cambridge, you are going to find out that fine lady's daughter's name and call her. You will tell her to come down here immediately. You, Agent Adams, will furnish transportation for her. There will be no excuses. No delays." His voice was low, his speech slow. Each word was spoken very clearly, very distinctly. He left no room for argument; his orders were to be carried out. "Her bill is to be taken care of by the Embassy, and an official letter of apology will be sent by Ambassador Ambrose." He suddenly turned away from them to return to Arlene Arbuckle's cubicle, then added in an even lower and more threatening voice," Get a doctor in there to see to her needs right now. And, I still have not forgotten about the long and serious talk that the three of us will have."

Half an hour later, while the doctors were giving her a thorough exam, her daughter and her son in law arrived by FBI transportation. An agent met them at the emergency room entrance and took them back to her curtained off area. "The doctor is just finishing up, and from what we've been told, she's going to be fine. Perhaps a little stiff from the fall

They did. Of course, it was, what happened. The agent explained to them that he could tell them that an attempt was made on an official guest's life, and that her mother had had the bad luck of being caught up in the murder plot. He was very sorry, but he could say no more, except that Mrs. Arbuckle was a fine and courageous lady. There were no more questions, so he left and took up his station at the entrance to the treatment area.

Agent Adams and Mr. Cambridge were at this moment in the executive offices of the hospital making secure phone calls thanks to the little electronic gadget that he had picked up earlier.

"Yes sir," Samantha was saying, "He will be fine … oh, the other victim? Yes, her name is Arlene Arbuckle … yes, yes, she's going to be fine, too. Actually sir, it was because of her location behind the Inspector that probably saved his life … no, I couldn't have placed myself anywhere else because of the crowd and still have been in position to either stop them before they did anything or capture them afterwards. Those were the orders of the British, off to one side and don't make a move until they do … yes, the Inspector did well to protect himself the way he did. Sir, I have to get back to him. I've already dictated my report to the local agents, and you'll be getting a finished copy, oh in," she held her left wrist up to her eyes and looked at her watch, "in the next hour. Thank you sir, goodbye."

'Well," she said hanging up the phone. "It's your tum. Mr. Noma is not a happy camper about my decision, but he knows that it was not my choice. I hope you have good luck on your end." Samantha turned around, opened the office door, and left, quietly closing it behind her. She went back down to the emergency room to see how Ulnar was doing.

Geoffrey placed his call to the Embassy. When the Ambassador was on the line Geoff requested that they go secure. Seconds later, it was safe for them to talk. "Mr. Ambassador, we've had some luck with the plan, but we almost lost Mr. Loop. If he had not been so quick, we would be facing some very embarrassing questions."

"What happened, Mr. Cambridge?"

Geoffrey told Ambassador Ambrose the entire story of what had happened in the depths of the subway station. From how the plan had developed, to how an extra number of people were there that had not been foreseen, to the push. He described Ulnar's quick thinking and the arrest of one of the felons.

"How many were there?"

"Unknown at this time, sir. What with the train and all of the confusion, you understand, people screaming, and running up to the edge of the platform trying to satisfy their morbid curiosity. Although Agent Adams did make mention of another man running up the stairs after she had caught the suspect."

"What about the other victim, Mrs..... Arbickle ... was it?"

"Arbuckle, sir. Mrs. Arlene Arbuckle and she's going to be fine. According to the Inspector, you will be sending a personal letter of apology. The Embassy will cover all hospital expenses, and make sure that she is given official transportation home after her release."

"Well, Mr. Cambridge, that does not surprise me. I was planning on doing so while you were telling me what had happened. And I'm going to phone the Foreign Office and request that an official apology comes from the Prime Minister's office, as well. After she's home, that is. And I am going to check to see if there is anything else we can do. When a member of an official government agency, such as this Embassy, is responsible for an injury to a citizen of the host country, whether by accident or on purpose, then that official should personally take care of it. In other words, taking responsibility for our own actions. I'm a firm believer in not hiding behind diplomatic immunity when I've done something wrong."

"Yes, Ambassador, I have heard that mentioned before. Oh, also before I forget, the Inspector is going to want a full account of our actions towards him since he came over here. He's finally caught on."

"Yes, well that was expected to happen, sooner or later. As I have said before, the man is no fool. We just hoped that it would be later. Let me see, there was something else…. Oh, Paul Cummings called. They believed the leak was one man. Intelligence has had a tail on him for the past twelve hours, although there is nothing to report yet. As soon as there is, I will get in touch with the three of you. I am also going to recommend that we leak today's failure on Ulnar's life. This will let them know that they are not supermen, that they make mistakes. I understand the pressure it puts on you, but I believe that you will be the first to understand that it is better to keep them off guard. Perhaps they will be pushed into making another error."

"Perhaps they will, sir. Don't forget, Ulnar will be held overnight for observation. They plan on releasing him around 12 noon tomorrow. We'll get some lunch and then finish our trip to Boston. Can you get in touch with our traveling Special Air Service chaps, George and Harry, and let them know of our change of plans?"

"I will. I'll also have your Commander leak the news about the one-day delay in the plans and also make new arrangements for the meeting with the Commissioner of Boston Police. Call me tomorrow afternoon after you settle into your hotel room."

"Will do, sir." Geoffrey sighed. He hung up the phone, took the electronic device off, and left the hospital's executive office. He went back down to the emergency room to begin a very long session with Inspector Ulnar Lewis Loop.

As he entered the curtained area that Ulnar had occupied, he noticed that only Sam was there. She explained to him that they finally assured Ulnar that everyone before him had been taken care of and that it was now his tum. "He's having his arm X rayed. If it's broken where they thought, and there are no complications, the doctor will put a cast on today."

"Is there anyone with him?"

One of our local agents is and he'll stay with him until he is ready to go to his room. We'll go there with him when it's time."

Thirty minutes later, one of the FBI Agents came for the two of them. He said that the Inspector had had a cast put on his arm and that he was being taken to his room. The agent also informed them that it had been a simple fracture to the radius bone. They asked how long he would be in a cast and were told that he had to be X rayed after five weeks to see how it was healing. Could any doctor perform that service, or must he return to this hospital, they asked. The agent said that Ulnar could have it done where he was at that particular time.

"Is there anything else that we need to know," Geoffrey asked.

"Not at this time," the agent replied.

"One more thing," Sam said just before they left for Ulnar's room. "We will need to change agents outside and inside his room every four hours. There will be a list of people who will be allowed to see him for his treatment. Check them thoroughly, we can't afford any more mistakes," They left to see the Inspector.

An hour outside of Boston, at a Roy Rodgers Restaurant just off of I-95, the leader of the assassination team was on a pay phone calling the person who hired him and his men. That person's name was unknown to them. All that he and his men knew, was that they were to rob the branch banks that were chosen for them. And of course for him and one other member of the team to travel to Philadelphia, and then New York, and try to murder the Inspector, making it look like an accident.

The phone rang three times, and then it was picked up. "Yes," a voice said.

"You're not who I have been talking to, who are you?"

"Who I am ain't none of your business. You were told to report to whoever answered this phone, or don't you wanna keep getting your money. Ya know that dough will help you buy the stuff you wanted."

"Okay, okay. I understand your point; however, you are not going to like my report ... "

Ulnar had been taken to his room and was under a mild sedation. An FBI agent was outside his room and another was just inside, sitting in a chair. Special Agent Samantha Adams and Geoffrey Cambridge were sitting in two chairs that were close to the bed and were talking to the Inspector.

His right arm was encased in a glow in the dark pink cast. The medication kept the pain down but allowed him to stay alert. He was glowering at the cast. "What in the world am I doing with this, *thing,* on my arm? Don't they have the old white plaster of paris concoction anymore?"

"Inspector, did you give anyone a hard time or happen to throw a tantrum while they were fixing you up?" Geoffrey asked. There was no answer. "I see… perhaps that will teach you to curb that temper. This is not England. Remember, the Americans consider this to be a type of humor."

You've made your point, now what about this attempt on my life?" He hesitated, then" Better yet just start from the beginning, Geoffrey."

"Sir, this story starts right after your retirement from the Yard. In fact, it was two weeks later that we received word from our underworld sources that you were marked for extinction; there is no better word for it… a team was on its way from Ireland to put you out of their misery from all the work you did on their bombing activities. We had records of them, including the latest pictures. They were intercepted at Heathrow Airport. However, just four months later, a second attempt was tried. This time it was stopped by the Constabulary in Larger Elfinwood.

We never knew of this attempted hit. There is no excuse, our underground stoolies never got wind of this attempt. But then, those bad lads got very careless. They found the area where you lived; however, not exactly where your cottage was located. So, they stopped at the station to ask directions. Apparently, this was to throw off any question as to their being legitimate friends. They said that they were old friends of yours and wanted to surprise you. Constable Correy was in the next office and heard the request. He summoned Sergeant Sanderson and the two of them, along with two other Constables, followed the men out of the village. About a kilometer from your place, they pulled them over and started to question them. These men did not know that all of your friends were known to the Yard, and therefore to Correy and Sanderson.

Now, before you get yourself in a snit," Geoff held up a hand to Ulnar, "These precautions were taken for your safety at the time of your retirement. And those two gentlemen of law enforcement were doing their jobs. Correy and Sanderson are not normal Constables working in the countryside. But instead, they are from the Special Branch and assigned there for your protection. Obviously for good reason."

"The three men in the vehicle were taken out of it bodily and put to the ground. A thorough search of the interior of the car and the boot came up with some very serious weapons. Two AK 4 7 s and a rocket propelled grenade launcher. There were five rockets for the RPG and ten, thirty round clips for the 47s."

"But Geoffrey, I never heard anything about these attacks, or even about any outcome in a court of law."

"That's quite easy to arrange, sir. First of all, you do not get any newspapers. You don't want to be bothered with the world's problems anymore. You don't even have a phone; besides, if you did, who would you call? You do not have any real friends outside of Scotland Yard. You have made yourself, for the last six of the nine months of retirement, a complete hermit. Furthermore, the three were arrested and tried on criminal charges for the weapons. And they were also wanted for bombings in London and Northern Ireland. There was no mention of you, and of course, they were not talking; not even to their own solicitor. Everything was kept quiet.

Although you were entitled to your retirement, you had too much to give to others. So, with the Queen's and the Prime Minister's approval, it was decided to get you involved with life, instead of your slowly rotting away at your estate. That was why you were sent on this trip. The fact that there is currently a series of robberies being committed in the Commonwealth of Massachusetts was just a lucky opportunity to help get you involved in life again. Don't you remember your attitude when you were first contacted for this trip?"

Ulnar looked at his two friends and thought back to the beginning of this trip and slowly nodded his head. "I haven't been the best of company, have I?"

"Sir, believe me, you have improved a great deal these last few days," Mr. Cambridge said. "However, back to cases.

At the beginning of this trip word came to us, again, that there was a price on your head. And it was over here, in America, that the price was going to be paid. Someone had learned of this trip and told an interesting party. This party has an extreme dislike of your being in America. He, or they, put this price on your head the moment you stepped on the plane for Washington. We believe that the other attempts on your life were to keep you from entering your old profession and traveling around the world helping others become as good as you are at the Science of Fingerprints. After they failed and you were told to come over here, then they decided to try again to take you out of the picture.

It wasn't until we found out about the bank jobs that it was decided that this was the reason for your life to be at risk. So, you were asked to help out with your expert knowledge. We were aware that you would have attempts on your life, and that we had to force their hand. After the try in Philadelphia, we, Agent Adams and myself, were ordered to stop in New York. Knowing full well that they would most likely try again. We took every precaution that we could and still not give our hand away. It worked; although it worked a little too well."

Geoffrey noisily cleared his throat, 'However, we did catch one of them and he is being held by Sam's people. It did not make the papers, yet. Someone will talk, but before then, they will know. There was another person in the team that tried to take you out, but he got away. He will report his failure. Moreover, the word is going to be put out into the underworld, and the delay in your travel plans will be leaked as well. Hopefully they will get angry at the miss and try again. We will be ready and with your help we might be able to…. What is the Americanism… oh, yes, to throw a monkey wrench into their plans, thus, getting us closer to the leaders of this crime wave."

"Why didn't you let me in on this from the beginning?"

"Again sir, because of your overall attitude. You did not want to come over here and therefore help out the Yard. What were the odds of you helping us to find out who no longer wanted you in the land of the living? So, the great plan. It has worked, so far, but as I said, we are not taking any more chances. They may come after you. With your help, we will be ready. Who knows, maybe we will be able to help solve the robberies as well."

"Geoff, you're right, I have been foolish. My wish for privacy has made me a recluse, but no longer. I realize, now, how ignorant I've been. I want to help you find these people who are after me. More importantly, though, I want to help people learn what I know … to give of myself for the betterment of the Science of Fingerprints."

"Sir, I am personally very glad to hear that; it will make all of our jobs that much easier." Sam said.

"But right now, I think that it is time to get some rest; the sedatives are taking effect, and I am going to need my rest. Goodnight. I'll see you two tomorrow."

"Goodnight, sir," they said in unison. The two of them turned to leave the room. Samantha made sure that both agents had their orders straight on her way out. They left the hospital and went to get some supper. Afterwards they went back to the Inspector's room to start making their plans for the afternoon trip to Boston. Three hours later Sam went to her room; they both needed their sleep.

The next day after Geoff and Agent Adams completed the plans and travel arrangements, they went to the hospital to get Ulnar. When they got to his room, they found him waiting on the bed. "Are you ready, sir?" Geoff asked.

"Yes, get me out of here."

"What's wrong; didn't you have a good night's sleep?" Sam asked.

"Yes, to that question also. No, it's the food; the last time I had food that tasted that bad was during the war."

Geoff asked, "Was that the Boer War, sir?"

"No, it was not," Ulnar said in mock anger. "Let me put it so that even you young, and oh so inexperienced, people can understand. The hearty man ate a condemned meal."

Neither one said anything more, although it was quite difficult to keep the laughter inside. They wanted to be sure that Ulnar was in good spirits. He was. The three of them left the hospital with the Inspector in the lead. He was in a wheelchair and was being pushed by one of the nurses. This time he was not difficult; he did not want any more American humor. They had a light lunch and then were on the road heading north to Boston.

The rest of the trip had no surprises. The weather held for most of the way, and it was only when they got near their destination that it started to get cloudy. The Inspector was very impressed by the countryside; he had already planned to visit different parts of the United States when this personal problem of his had been brought to a satisfactory end. By the time they had reached downtown, the skies had opened up and it was pouring rain with the bucket.

When they pulled up in front of the main entrance to the hotel, they discovered that the unloading area in front of the lobby doors was packed full of cars. The three of them got out of the vehicle as fast as possible and made a mad dash for cover. Ulnar tried desperately to keep his cast dry. Once they were out of the rain, they located the valet service and a bell hop. Agent Adams made arrangements for the luggage to be unloaded and the car parked. Then Ulnar, Geoffrey, and Samantha went in to register.

Ulnar had accidentally hit his cast on the door frame of the car in his hurry to get into a dry area; so, when they got to their rooms, he took a pain pill. Besides, it had been a long trip and the other two were also tired. Geoffrey called for room service so that they could relax. After supper Geoff made his call to the Ambassador to let him know that they had arrived without any problem. There was still no more news on the possible leak at the Yard and the meeting was on for nine the following morning. The three of them went to bed early so that they would be at their best the following day.

After a restful night and a good breakfast early the next morning, they had the valet get their car and then drove through the misty rain to the headquarters of the Boston Police Department for their nine-a.m. meeting with the Commissioner. A minute after they had been ushered into the gentleman's office, Harry Smythe and George Black were also brought into the room. The Commissioner got up from his specially made chair and came around his desk to greet everyone.

Perry S. Swordes was a large bear of a man who towered over everyone in the room, even the SAS men, who are not known for being small in size. He stood at six feet nine inches and weighed approximately two hundred and ninety pounds. His large hands swallowed each of the others' when he shook them. His deep bass voice matched his size.

"Good morning, everyone. It is indeed a pleasure to meet all of you," he said as he gestured for them to take their seats. "Especially you, Inspector. I've heard a great deal about you and your work in the Science of Fingerprints. By the way, how is your arm," he asked pointing to the bright cast. "Your Ambassador filled me in on what has happened to you since you started your trip from Washington.

"It's fine, thank you. Just a little pain is all." Ulnar said as he looked around the office, noticing the usual pictures with celebrities and the degrees in law enforcement and business management from a leading university. He also noted that this man had once worked in uniform; there were several awards for his work in cleaning up the criminals from the streets. "Pardon, me? Sorry, I was woolgathering again."

"I said that it is my understanding that one of the men was captured."

"Yes, that's quite true. Agent Adams did a superb job in doing so. Although, we haven't heard anything about him, yet."

While this conversation was going on, George Black pulled out his notebook from an inside jacket pocket, flipped past some pages until he came to the one's he wanted. He leaned slightly forward in his chair and cleared his throat. "Ahem ... excuse me, gentlemen. I was in touch with the Ambassador very early this morning." He looked at Special Agent Samantha Adams and said, "Your FBI chaps are still funneling the needed information through him; he related to me that the poor excuse for a hit man has no fingerprint records in this country. The prints, as I understand it, were sent to West Virginia, where a computer known as the ... FINDER system?"

She nodded her head and said," Yes, it stands for Fingerprint Reader."

"Well," he continued, "it did a complete search of the prints in minutes. However, they are going to send the prints by special courier to Scotland Yard. They will in turn forward a copy to INTERPOL (International Police). Perhaps we'll hear something on it later."

"Wait a minute," Commissioner Swordes said. "If the fellow that was caught and fingerprinted didn't have a record with your organization, wouldn't that mean that he wasn't from the U.S.? Wouldn't that mean that he was from Ireland?"

"Not necessarily, Commissioner," said Ulnar. "Fingerprints that are taken and sent to a central clearing house are not always the best. Many times, it's because the people are not properly trained to take them. In other cases, it's because the people do not care."

"What does that have to do with taking fingerprints or with fingerprint records for that matter? They show it on crime shows and, in the movies; it doesn't look that difficult," Perry said.

"Yes, I've seen your American television crime shows and some of your movies. If someone actually had to classify and compare those prints, he would throw them out and ask for another set. And, if they went to a clearinghouse, those people would return the fingerprint card to the contributor.

Sir, if there is any slippage of the fingers, or if there is too much ink, or too little, then those prints will be unclassifiable. The classifier must be able to tell the pattern types and see the ridge characteristics."

"What are ridge characteristics?"

"You might call them points, which I believe is short for points of identity," the Inspector continued. "I have only heard the term referred to as points on your television shows. A more common term that is used by fingerprint people is Friction Ridge Detail. A term named after Sir Francis Galton, who in the late 1800's wrote a book entitled Fingerprints, was Galton's Details.

Regardless of the term, it is these characteristics that can show the difference between two fingers, or patterns, or even feet. Basically, it is the type of characteristic, its position in reference to the others, and the number of them.

So. If the fingerprints were returned for any reason, there would not be a record."

"There is a second reason," Samantha said. "He may not have been arrested for DUI or a felony. Outside of people arrested for those crimes, we don't keep non felony arrests. They're returned to the contributing agency."

"It doesn't help a bit, does it?" Perry Swordes asked.

"No sir, it doesn't. We'll just have to await word from either Scotland Yard or **INTERPOL**," Agent Adams answered. "By the way, sir, have there been any new leads?"

"Nothing so far. However, we've been fortunate, or maybe unfortunate depending on your point of view, because there have been no other robberies since the bungled bank robbery in Smaller Wormwood. By the way, it was another branch of the Paul Revere Bank. That's the one where they put a rider on every loan ... " His voice trailed off, as all the heads in the room turned towards him in surprise.

"Mmm, sorry, couldn't resist a little local humor. A play on the historical event." He became serious again. "Besides that, one, and the branch of the 181 Bank of Boston and the main branch of the Paul Revere Bank here in town, there were two branches of the Third Trust Bank of Sommerset, and a branch of the Merchant Marine Bank of New England, and a branch of the 9th Savings and Loan of Overton. The Smaller Wormwood job is the only one that they botched. And an interesting fact about these robberies has surfaced during the intense investigation. The banks are all part and parcel of the Teme family's holdings. Of course, they don't own the banks outright, but they are the principal stockholders in all of them. The head of the family, James Terne III is now retired; however, his son Cuspal is now running the family's affairs."

"Who?" Samantha asked.

"His full name is Cuspal Patrick Terne. It's a very old New England family. They came over to the Mayflower ... made their money first as merchants, and later in shipping. There were rumors that part of the shipping trade was legal, you know, spices, silks, tea ... trade in East India and the orient. The other trade was in slaves. But there is no way to prove it and that family of course would completely reject such a notion. Even the father, James ill, was said to be quite the cutthroat in business, and it has been whispered about in the lower, criminal element, that in his early days he involved part of his shipping fleet in bringing the good Canadian whiskies into the U.S. A rumrunner, if you will. Again, not something that the family would acknowledge. Back to the current family.

Cuspal was brought up in all of the right private schools. Made excellent grades, and even majored in business at Harvard. Graduated a year early, I understand. He's been running the holdings for a number of years and has also, through very shrewd mergers and acquisitions, expanded the family businesses well beyond what they were. Currently, he is CEO of several corporations, and he sits on the boards of four others. These are in addition to the banks and other business ventures."

"Sounds like a very successful and powerful man." Geoffrey Cambridge said. "Is there any reason that they are choosing his banks? I take it that only the banks that his family have an interest in have been hit and no others." It was a statement, not a question.

"No, no others. As I said, an interesting sidelight of the investigation."

"Do you know anything else about the robberies, Commissioner Swordes?" Agent Adams asked.

"No more than has already been reported to the bureau. On each of the robberies, there were four men." He said referring to the notes on his desk. "We believe that there are more than those in the gang."

"Are you sure?"

"There's a good chance of it being true," replied Swordes. "The group we are looking for have, or at least some of them do, Irish accents and speak what is believed to be Gaelic. Now, being Boston, this is not unheard of; so, we don't know if they're American citizens, or if they're from Ireland and are in this country illegally. However, since the captured criminal has the same accent, he is probably with the robbers. Your people, Agent Adams, are sending a photo of him which we'll show to our bank victims. And we're going to send a copy of the descriptions of the robbers to New York, as well as an artist's drawing of all the bank suspects given to us by the victims. Your New York office is going to enter those, and the photo of your man Inspector, then add a hat and sunglasses. By trying it from both ends, maybe we'll see if that will get us any closer to solving this mess."

The Inspector turned his head to the left to say something to Geoffrey, but it died in his throat. There was a look of intense concentration on his face. "Something amiss, Geoff?"

He looked back at Ulnar. "Sorry, sir. Something that the commissioner said reminded me of something else, but I can't remember who said it or exactly what it was. Perhaps it will come back to me."

Perry Swordes continued his report to the gathered specialists. "All of the descriptions of the robbers matched two of the bank jobs. Those were the two here, in Boston. Yet, two of those ... ," he thumbed through the reports, " ... ah, here they are. Two of those matched with the robbery at the 9th Savings and Loan of Overton. But they didn't match up with the two robberies at the Third Trust Bank of Sommerset. The other two from here appeared to be the same as the men involved with those two robberies. Going through these reports shows that they have tried to team up in such a manner that it would throw us off track. Obviously, it hasn't worked quite as well as they probably would have liked."

He carefully continued through his case notes. "Oh, here's something that I almost missed. In the branch of the Merchant Marine Bank of New England and the branch of the Third Trust Bank of Sommerset that was first hit, the surveillance cameras were not working. The first one had no film, and the other was down for repair."

"How could that be? I thought that they had to be operational at all times." Agent Adams interrupted.

"No, not really. In fact, the one that broke down did so at just about the time the bank closed on the previous day. In the case of the Third Trust Bank, the film had been on order for two weeks. It didn't get to the bank until the day after the robbery."

"What about the one that failed?"

The Commissioner checked through his papers. "Mmm ... let's see ... ah yes. Our investigators checked it out and found that it was just a normal failure. There was no sign of tampering. That's probably why they're hitting the smaller branches of these banks. The take is much smaller of course, but the chance of the cameras not working is increased. So, right now we don't have much to go on except the descriptions. We're also hoping that they will mess up somewhere and leave some type of additional evidence ... oh, that reminds me."

He searched through the files again. "Here. At the Paul Revere Bank robbery in town, one of the suspects stepped into something wet in the street and tracked it into the bank. Got some nice photographs of the shoe print. The investigator in charge of the case is writing it down now. When we get anything, I'll give you a call."

"That's it. Thank you all for coming in today." Perry Swordes stood up; this signaled the end of the meeting.

"It's been a pleasure meeting you, sir," Samantha spoke for every one of the visitors. "Here's the name of our hotel, and my room number. And if we hear anything more from our side, we'll be in touch."

They all said goodbye, left the room, took the elevator to the main floor, and left the building in silence. By this time the rain had stopped, but the sky was still overcast. There was nothing else they could do now except keep an eye on Ulnar Loop.

Sam and Ulnar continued on to their vehicle. Geoffrey stopped just outside the main doors and held out his arms so he could stop George Black and Harry Smythe.

"I don't see a need for you two to be here any longer. We've got the threat against the Inspector's life covered, and your informant is no longer in the land of the living. I'm going to send you back to the Yard. See if you can help Commander Cummings with the person who is speaking out of tum." He shook their hands. "It has been a pleasure working with you two young men."

"Thank you sir," they said in return; then they left. George and Harry drove back to the Churned Up Inn and got their clothes and luggage carriers. Two hours later they were on a plane back to London.

CHAPTER FIVE

When Geoffrey left the Boston Police Department, he took out the slip of paper that contained the Inspector's measurements. He had gotten them when he had last talked to the Commander. He went shopping.

A few hours later he returned to the hotel with two armloads of purchases. He kicked at the bottom of the door with his right foot; he placed his right ear to the door to hear if there was any noise coming from inside. There was no sound. He kicked again. He placed his ear against the door for a second time. Listening, he heard a faint noise and voices. He lowered his packages to the hallway floor and took out his weapon. Just as he was getting ready to kick open the door, he heard the locks being undone. The door was opened a crack.

Special Agent Samantha Adams peeked out through the crack at Geoffrey. "Welcome back, stranger," she said.

"Is everything alright?" he asked, trying to peer through the tiny crack and past Sam's head.

"Yes, of course. Why do you ask?"

"Well... ," he started to say as he bent over to reclaim his bags and boxes from his shopping tour, his weapon now safely put away. "No one answered the door when I knocked. What with the Inspector's safety being my main concern and all, I suspected that something might be amiss, so ... ", he finished after he had regained the parcels.

Samantha opened the door fully and stood to one side so that Geoff could enter his room. "So," she picked up on his statement, "You decided to pull out your weapon and kick down the door. For heaven's sake, he was in my room watching the news. He had become lonely and needed the company. Although he didn't come right out and say it, I believe that with all those months of living alone at his country cottage were actually starting to get at him. Now he enjoys seeking out company."

She continued telling Geoffrey what the two of them had been doing while awaiting his return from his errands. Relieved that everything was okay, he set his passle of parcels on the bed as she finished her report. The two of them continued on through the connecting door and into her room. They found Ulnar engrossed in a program that was dedicated to describing all of the flora and fauna that could be found in different sections of New England.

"You do know, sir, that sitting that close to the set could possibly ruin your eyes." Geoffrey said with a hint of mischief showing in his eyes.

"What can you do with someone like him anyway?" Sighed Sam as she crossed the room and sat down at the foot of her bed. "He's just doing as he pleases. He doesn't listen to anyone anymore. I suppose that comes with getting older. You just become cantankerous."

Ulnar turned his head towards Samantha. Geoffrey crossed in front of her to sit in the upright chair at the writing desk on the same side of the room. "What are you two children," he emphasized the last word, 'Blathering about now? I was enjoying the show very much until you started raising some sort of fuss in the background. Didn't your parents ever teach you any manners?" He asked.

"Look at this respect that we get. We try to look out for his best interests, and he sits there and insults us," Geoffrey said. "I just don't know if all of this work in keeping him safe is worth the effort. Not only ours, mind you, but the people back at Scotland Yard; the young officers back in New York; and also, all of those agents that Samantha called in. Look how fast they got to the scene to help him. And what about that poor woman…," he finished, shaking his bowed head in mock sadness, and pretending that there was too much hurt in him to continue.

After a moment he raised his head and looked at Samantha and Ulnar. They were both wearing large grins. Almost as large as the one he was wearing.

"Seriously, sir," Geoff continued, "Please remember that when you leave our room for another, leave the connecting doors open so that you can hear anyone trying to enter the other room."

The Inspector asked what all of this was about, so Geoffrey told him about his knocking on the door to their room. He explained about his concern that something may have happened to the two of them and that more care must be taken.

"I'm sorry, Geoffrey. I just did not think about my actions in that manner."

"Actually," Samantha added, "I didn't think of it either. I was here and knew that nothing was going to happen. I just didn't take into consideration that you would act that way. He was safe, and you had your key. I didn't consider that your hands would be full and would need help getting in. I'll be much more careful in the future."

"I have a confession to make. This is one of the reasons that you were chosen for this assignment. As I told you a few days ago, I have seen your record. You should be commended on the fine job that you have done in fighting bank robbers, the mob, and other assorted misfits in crime. Your record of assignments, including your current one at the FBI headquarters, shows your career to be on the fast track.

However, I was informed, and this is one reason for your current assignment, that for this job a great deal of tact was needed. Not," he added holding up his hand to ward off any possible interruption, "That you don't have any. It's to see how much and to give you training in protecting diplomats and other VIPs."

"Like me?" Inquired the Inspector.

"Yes sir, just like you."

"Well, I say. I'm very glad to hear this bit of news. At least I am not here just to be the brunt of your childish attempts at humor."

Geoffrey shook his head and continued with his talk to Samantha. "I'm not supposed to say, but there is talk that a satisfactory completion of this trip will open up your career to a new level, Agent Adams. When I used the term fast track to describe your career, it was not being misused."

"Thank you, Geoffrey, for this news. I had no idea, but then no one ever hears something like this. All anyone can do is just keep on going and pray that all of their hard work will come to be recognized.

"Well now. That's settled; how about a spot of dinner. I'm becoming frightfully hungry." Ulnar Loop said.

With that announcement, things settled down for the trio. During the next week, Geoff and Sam kept a very close eye on the Inspector. There was no news of any more bank robberies in the surrounding towns that matched the M.O. of the previous ones and nothing on the shoeprint. So, the three of them decided to take a busman's holiday while they waited for something to break. This started on the day after their visit with the Police Commissioner, Perry Swordes.

It was the first day that the weather cleared up. That first morning before they took Ulnar out, consisted of a sky that was a very deep blue, with the occasional white fluffy cloud passing overhead. The temperature topped out at only 80 degrees, and because of a light breeze coming from Boston Harbor, this was just right.

Since Ulnar and Geoff had never been to Boston, Agent Adams gave them the fifty-cent tour. The Boston Field Office had been her first big assignment, so she knew all the sights that visitors liked to see. They followed the Freedom Trail; she showed them the Old North Church,

Paul Revere's House, the Boston Massacre Site, and the Custom House. They walked through the Waterfront Park and enjoyed a nice lunch outside. They even found some nurseries for Ulnar to walk through. This gave him a chance to sample firsthand some of the several varieties of plant life in the area.

Back at Scotland Yard, George and Harry were receiving orders from Commander Cummings. "We are going to leak a false message to our informant about the Inspector. It will sound so important that our tattle tale will make his move as soon as he can find an excuse."

"What is the message going to be, and who will deliver it?" George Black asked.

"You will; no one except me knows that you two are back. Besides, you are unknown to most of the people here, except, that is, as voices over the telephone. And, as a voice, Mr. Black, you will phone in the misleading message through the normal channels.

Our man will hear it, make an excuse to leave work, and run his little errand. You gentlemen will follow him and report back directly to Robert MacGregor about anyone he meets. He and his men will be standing by to go to your location and affect an arrest. Here are your radios which are already set on the correct frequency. Your call sign will be Fox Hound and the arrest team will be Hunting Team."

"Can we expect any trouble from the subject?" Asked Harry.

"No, I don't think you will. This is not a man of great bravery. He is just greedy."

Two hours later, George placed the call to the Commander.

"Scotland Yard, Welsley speaking."

"Welsley, put me through to Commander Cummings, please. I have some news to pass to him about the Inspector."

"The Inspector… is he alright?"

"Well, yes and no. Just put me through to the Commander please."

"This is Commander Cummings. Yes Constable, by all means, put him through." After a few minutes George was on the line. "Yes, Mr. Black and how is everything going over there in the colonies?"

"Things are fine, sir. Well, that is, except for the Inspector."

"Oh? Not bad news I hope."

"Nothing serious. It's just his arm. And his age. The two are not getting along with one another. It's giving him quite some pain and he doesn't like the weather. It isn't helping that it is too warm, and his arm is swelling inside the cast. The doctors here suggest that he go back to England to recuperate at his estate, Twinned Loop. He will be completely healed in a few more weeks. Then if nothing has been solved over here, he can come back."

"Oh, dear me, I'm sorry to hear that. Will he be requiring any special treatment or protection while he is home?"

"No, sir. We don't believe so. The threat to him over here should be over. After all, we have captured the man who tried to murder him. And it is the belief of everyone here that it is not a conspiracy. Just the one man with some sort of grudge against the old gent. Of course, that one man is not talking, but they believe he will eventually."

"That is good news. So, when do you expect him to leave?"

"Day after tomorrow. He'll leave on a 7 AM flight to London. After that, he will continue on to the estate."

"Very good. I'll see to it that he gets a ride. Thank you for calling with this news Mr. Black. And good luck with the rest of your assignment

"Thank you, sir." George rang off. Nothing to do now, he thought, except to wait. He and Harry were good at that. All of those years involved in special assignments for the Special Air Service taught them well. George had the west entrance to the building covered, and Harry had the north entrance sewed up. Now there was nothing more they could do until their quarry left on his evil errand.

Ninety minutes later, their suspect did exactly that. He scurried out of the west entrance and hailed a cab. George was ready for that and had one already hired. He radioed Harry. "He's on his way. I'm in a cab headed south. I'll keep you informed. Out."

The cab carrying the Commander's personal secretary, Constable William Welsley, headed straight for an entrance to the underground that was about a kilometer away. He paid the driver and got out of the cab. George went out a block away. Harry pulled up in another cab and joined him. "He's going down into the station. Nine will get you ten that his greed is overriding his caution. He never once looked back or tried to see if he had a tail."

"Why should he?" Asked Harry. "He's never believed that he would get caught. After all, he was the Commander's secretary for many years. He was put in that position by certain higher ups because of his political savvy. No one would ever suspect him."

"Yes, except for this trip that the Inspector made. And the Commissioner of the Yard had all of those people put under a microscope. That's the only way that we found out that this gentleman was living far beyond his means. I cannot believe how he flaunted his newfound funds. I wonder though, how long has he been doing this?"

Harry said, "It doesn't matter anymore. We're going to put a sudden halt to his misdeeds. And possibly catch someone else in the act as well."

They entered the underground by means of a long stairway. There were a number of people using it on this day, but not so many that Harry and George could not keep track of their quarry. Black and Smythe watched from the back of the crowd that was waiting for the train to come.

As they watched him, they could not believe that he was so calm. There was no doubling back to check for a tail during the cab ride. He didn't suddenly stop and looked in a shop window. Welsley wasn't even looking around at the surrounding people to see if anyone looked familiar. This man was either not very smart or he was very sure of himself because of his position at Scotland Yard.

George decided that it was a combination of the two, which made the Constable very stupid; thus, he would be easy to follow. He also knew that the people that this man was reporting to were not stupid. He and Harry would have to be on their toes while they followed him. Those other people would know how Welsley was coming to the rendezvous. They would more than likely keep an eye out for anyone who looked like they were paying too much attention to their stoolies.

These thoughts were cut short when the train arrived. The crowd moved forward to board. Their man pushed his way onto the car directly in front of him. George and Harry split up. During the wait for the train, they had given no hint of knowing one another. Hopefully, it would fool anyone who was watching and looking for something out of the ordinary.

George entered the car in front of Welsley's and walked to the back of that car. Harry entered the one behind and took up station near the front of his car. From here, they could keep the Constable under complete view without giving anything away. Both men were very careful not to be obvious in keeping their quarry contained.

William Welsley turned to the right as he entered the train. He found an empty seat and sat down. There was an abandoned copy of the Dailey Mirror on the seat next to him. He picked it up and started to thumb through the gruesome pictures and stories. This kept the man busy and easy to keep under surveillance. The trip on the train was not a. quick one. They rode for what was close to an hour with a good number of stops. Finally, at the end of that time the train slowed down for the last stop on the line. Their man put down the paper and got ready to get off at the stop.

The train slowed and jerked to a stop with a squeal of brakes. Everyone that was on the train got up and crowded at the doors of the cars. Harry did the same in his car, being the first to disembark. The doors opened and the mass of humanity crushed and crowded their way onto the platform. Harry was off to one side as William left his car. A few minutes later George was also on the platform seemingly not to be in a hurry while at the same time doing just that. He caught up to Smythe, leaving a small group of people between him and Harry. In this manner they emerged from the Underground behind the Constable. When they gained the cracked, worn, and neglected sidewalk, they found themselves near the docks that lined the Thames River. The always present odors that came off the river on the breeze were almost gagging. Welsley took out a handkerchief from his suit's breast pocket and briefly, daintily held it to his mouth and nose; then he put it away being very careful to breathe through his mouth.

George and Harry, who had already gotten rid of their sports jackets, were now mussing their hair, and trying to fit in with some of the better dressed people in the area. Because of their service in some very bad places in the world, they did not have any problem getting used to those docksides and riverbank odors of dead fish, oil, grease, diesel fuel, and raw sewage. Harry crossed to the other side of the street from Welsley and got ahead of him. George remained behind him on the same side and behind a group of locals. When it looked like it might be a fairly good walk, they started to carefully change places with one another.

This went on for several blocks. Suddenly, the Constable stopped, turned to his left, and entered a cheap, rundown, even for this area of the city, hotel. His followers also stopped. George motioned for Harry to hurry to the end of the block and go down the alley so that he could take up station outside the back entrance if there was one. As Harry worked his way through the garbage strewn alley to the trash laden back entrance of the cheap hotel, George entered the front entrance and walked over to the man behind the desk. "Which room did the man who just entered go to?"

"What man?" The skinny, pimply faced, dirty young man asked.

Right away, George knew that he would be getting very little cooperation from this weasel. Pulling himself up to his full height, he looked down on the desk clerk. Putting his ham sized hands on the desk, he asked the young fool, once again.

"I don't know who you're talking about, mate." The clerk responded, this time a little nervously. He stood there, with his head up, trying desperately not to be frightened. Pimple face reminded George of a little bantam rooster pretending that it was in charge of the barnyard when in reality it was surrounded by full sized roosters.

Mr. Black stood there, a full foot above the now jittery clerk. "Fine." He replied with an evil, confident grin on his face. He pulled out his radio. "Fox Hound to Hunting Team."

"Hunting Team here, Fox Hound," replied the leader of the capture team. "Have you cornered the quarry?"

'We have him inside the Winston Arms; it's down by the docks ... " He was cut off.

"Yes, we know where it is. However, it will take us about thirty minutes to get there. Can you detain him if he decides to leave before that time, Fox Hound?"

"Roger, Hunting Team. In fact, I am just about to convince the manager of this fine establishment that it would be in his best interests to answer my question." He took his finger off of the send button and looked down at the now petrified clerk. "Isn't that right little man; or do I have to relearn some of my training in tongue loosening?" George Black was a persuasive man. Captain George Black of the Special Air Service in full intimidation, was, indeed, a very persuasive man.

By now the skinny, pimply faced, dirty young clerk was empty of all courage. "Yes Sir! He went up to room 320. That's on the third floor, fourth room on the left." He spoke so fast that much of what he said was slightly slurred.

Captain Black switched channels on the radio. "Harry?"

"Yes, George," was the reply.

"Are you in the back of the building, at the rear entrance?"

Harry looked around in his immediate area. "If you mean this filthy, rodent infested alley way, outside a back door, that resembles so many third world countries, yes, I am. Do you need me for anything important? That is, more than standing out here in this smelly garbage."

"Yes, Leftenant Smythe; if you are done with the small and disturbingly cheap travelogue of the alley, I would appreciate your presence here, in what passes for a lobby. Do you copy?"

"That I do Captain. I'll be there in ... oh, fifteen seconds."

Twenty seconds later Harry joined George in the tiny lobby. "You're late, Harry."

"Sorry, George. Now, what's up?"

"We have orders to stay here and hold the guests upstairs until the Hunting Team can arrive. That will be in about twenty-five minutes."

"In other words, we're the ones that must go up and take care of business. Just like the old days, sir; we can only rely on ourselves."

"You're wrong on that, Leftenant. This time, we had an entire city to cover, and we do have help. Now, you take the lift, and I will take the stairs. First, though, let's get ready. We don't know what is waiting up there for us." The two commandos took their shirt tails out of their pants. Strapped around their mid sections were their weapons of choice. Two nine-millimeter weapons.

They took them out. Harry rang for the lift, and George started up the stairs. This was done to cover any possible lapses in intelligence. If the meeting upstairs had ended early, George and Harry knew that at least one of the participants would be heading down. Which way was anybody's guess. So, they split up. The elderly lift slowly shook and shuddered on its way to the third floor. At the same time George quietly crept up the old, splintered stairs.

George stepped quietly through the fire door from the stairs; at the same time Harry left the lift. They met each other just outside the elevator, and together, continued silently down the hallway to room 320. George crossed to the opposite side of the doorway. They stood outside of the room in question and listened. The two of them could hear voices from inside which meant that their quarry was still inside. Along with a mystery guest.

WHAM! WHAM! WHAM! George's big beefy hand rammed itself into the cheap wooden door. At the same time Harry spun outwards into the hall, his right foot poised upwards. That same foot went crashing into the door with the knob. It splintered into several pieces. Those pieces went flying into the room. The two men that were, up until then, having a relatively quiet talk, suddenly looked up, all conversation having ceased. Constable William Welsley and the man he was visiting, barely escaped being hit by the splinters.

Black and Smythe quickly entered the cheap room and spread apart; their weapons, grasped by both hands, were stretched out in front of them. George ordered in a voice that would have stopped a law-abiding citizen's heart, **"FREEZE, PEOPLE."**

George pointed his nine-millimeter at Welsley and Harry pointed his at the other man. The two occupants of the ill-furnished room raised their hands as if they knew the routine by force of habit.

"I say, what is the meaning of this rude interruption?" Welsley asked in a high quavering voice. Trying to be much braver than he felt, he added, "I will have you know that I am a representative of her majesty's government; I am involved in very secret dealings with a defector from the IRA which you are not endangering. Put your weapons away at once! If you do not, I will be forced to report you to the highest authorities!" He squeaked.

During this conversation, the questionable gentleman from Ireland started to move very slowly to one side, while Harry's attention was drawn away from him. At the same time, he dropped his hand to the small of his back.

"Never mind the fairy tales, sir," replied Harry, who was still being distracted. "I happen to know this person with whom you are conversing, and he is no defector. He is responsible for killing a large number of women and children during the past two years. His bombs have put a great many people on the welfare rolls because of the damage done to English families. The drug problem in the Americas could do no more harm than he has with his explosions." In a very deadly voice, he added, "And if you do not move away from him, I will feel no guilt in taking you when I take him."

"What do you mean?" The Constable nearly blubbered.

Taking advantage of the distraction, the Irish bomber quickly pulled his weapon from the back waistband of his trousers. The weapon, grasped in both hands, came up and ...

George's weapon made a deafening explosion in the confines of the small, cheap room. The bomber went down crying in pain from the wound that was low in his shoulder. His nine-millimeter clattered across the bare wooden floor of the room.

"COVER ME, LEFTENANT," Captain Black ordered in a loud, commanding voice to Smythe. At the same time, he took two large paces to his left and put the hot barrel of his weapon to the Irishman's head. "Do not move, sir, or I will be forced to do something that I would prefer not to do.

Any fight that was left in the bomber's body, had already left him. He lay very still and defeated. He knew how lucky he was to be alive; these people did not shoot to wound. In fact, George was stunned at his aim. "Dear me, Harry. I can't believe that I missed it so badly. By the way, next time keep a closer eye on your prisoner. Your actions in this matter will not make a young Leftenant into an old Captain."

Harry crossed over to take charge of William Welsley. He was too much of a professional to let a critique of his performance interfere with his job. He curtly ordered the informant to lie down on his stomach and to put his hands behind his head with the fingers interlaced. The hollow man complied with the order; there was no fight left in him.

When the Hunting Team arrived at room 320 fifteen minutes later, they found the suspects and Fox Hound in the same positions. "Here they are, sir." Harry reported promptly.

"Good job me...," the leader of the special arrest team from Scotland Yard started to say. "Do you know who you have here?" He asked in quiet surprise after seeing who the captured man was.

"I do sir," Harry replied before George could answer. "This is Liam Mahr, Captain. As I was saying before I became stupid, he was the leader of a large gang of the IRA terrorists. He was also against my platoon's presence in Dub ... "

"Yes, and you know why, you dirty sneaking commando. You helped get rid of many of my people with your tactics." Liam interrupted.

"Thank goodness for that," Hunting Team leader said. "Take these ... *men* ... away and put them under the tightest security that we have available," he said to his men. "We'll take it from here, gentlemen." He added George and Harry.

As his men handcuffed the two criminals, Liam Mahr cried out, "Watch out for my shoulder you oafs. I've been wounded, remember, and I require medical attention. I do have my rights."

The Hunting Team leader agreed, "Right you are Mahr; you do have your right to medical attention, and you shall have it. We take very good care of anyone that we injure, which, I might add, is more than you do for your victims. Take this scum out of my sight," he added. He turned his attention back to George.

"By the way, how did you miss?" Hunting Team leader asked.

"An unlucky shot, sir." Was all George would say.

The leader looked at George with a steady stare. Captain Black returned the look with no hint of embarrassment. They both knew that the Irish bomber would not talk, but he would endure many an uncomfortable year in the custody of the English. Of course, even if he did not say one word, his capture might signal a new era in negotiations with the other terrorists in Ireland. No terrorist can stand the fact that one of his own might talk. The Americans had the same problem with the mob. According to the papers, the mob was losing the battle; so, would the Irish Terrorists, eventually. After all, good almost always overcomes bad; regardless of what is seen and heard in the news.

George and Harry contacted Commander Cummings, who said that he would like to see them back in his office as soon as their paperwork was finished. When they arrived, he ushered them in and invited them to take a seat. He went to the intercom and spoke to his new temporary personal aide, asking for her to bring in some tea.

The tea arrived, hot and very welcome, two minutes later. "Captain, Leftenant, I want to thank you both for all of your help in this case. I know, I know, it doesn't seem like that much, but you carried out each of your assignments in an outstanding manner. Especially, when you helped take down the former Constable, William Welsley and that Mahr chap. In fact, I have been in touch with your commanding officer and have told him as much. We have agreed that a written commendation along with moving your names up to the top of your respective promotion lists would be a nice way of thanking you. Of course, the Prime Minister would have to agree with this, but we don't see a problem with that. Unless ... hrumph ... you decide to foul up in some grand manner.

George and Harry set their tea down, both of them with identical looks of surprise on their faces. George was the first to get himself under control and with a straight face, he said, "No, Commander. I'm not planning on doing anything of that nature in the future. Are you, Harry?"

''Nor me, sir.'' Harry replied, equally straight faced.

''I thought not,'' said Cummings. ''Well then, I believe that will be all. Transportation will be arranged for you back to your command.''

The three men finished their tea. As Black and Smythe were about to leave the office, the Commander said with his own straight face, "Oh by the way, I almost forgot to tell you the rest of the news.

You've both been granted thirty days leave to visit your families. I understand that it has been awhile ... hmm," he said, consulting a paper on his cluttered desk, "Almost a year since your last leave. Enjoy it gentlemen." He said with a mischievous grin on his face.

Harry and George looked at each other and then at the Commander. They smiled back at him, knowing full well that he had pulled his own little joke on them. As they left the office to arrange transport to their families and start a well-earned rest, Harry turned his head toward George and asked a very good question. "I wonder if the Inspector and his crowd have made any headway in solving those robberies since we've been gone?"

A week after the arrest of the former Constable and Liam Mahr, the IRA bomber, there was still no more headway made on the bank robberies. There also had been no other robberies or evidence collected on the existing cases. It was as if the gang were gathering its strength for a new wave of crime. Samantha, Geoffrey, and Ulnar continued to follow up on any leads that were passed to them, but even they came no closer to solving these cases. Then one afternoon the phone rang in Samantha's room. It was Bill Williams, the Special Agent in Charge of the Boston Field Office.

"Special Agent Samantha Adams," she said, answering the phone.

"Sam, this is Bill Williams down at the Boston field office. S.A.D. Noma called to inform you of the change involving the lines of communication. You will now receive your orders from Washington through me. If you have anything to give to them, you are to send it through me at this office. I'm to be your liaison; this includes anything the Boston P.O. will have for you."

"Why the change, Bill?"

"I asked that same question myself He wants the three of you to be able to follow any leads or hunches of your own without being tied down in one place. This gives us a firsthand account of anything that happens without any possible filtering out of information."

"Come on, Bill, that sort of thing doesn't happen anymore. After all, we're one big happy law enforcement family; aren't we? You know that personal glory doesn't enter into major cases anymore. At least, not within the bureau." She finished with a straight face. Getting back to the subject of the call, she asked, "Anything else?"

"Yeah, Sam, there is. They got the informant. Your Mr. Cambridge will fill you in after he calls Commander Cummings. The reason, and you can tell him, for his calling Cummings and not the Ambassador, is because of the arrest. They feel that there will be no more leaks about your travels, and the bureau agrees." After a moment of silence, 'Well, that's all. Take care of yourselves and don't forget to call me if you need anything."

"I will, Bill. And thank you." She hung up the phone and passed along the message about the capture.

"Great!" exclaimed Geoffrey. Ulnar heartily agreed with that and felt as if a large weight had been lifted from his seventy-year-old shoulders.

"Now all I have to do is get rid of this horrible cast," he complained.

"Temper, temper, Inspector. Remember how and why you got it to begin with." Geoffrey reminded him. Then, "Okay!" He said briskly clapping his hands together once. "I'll call the Commander and get our orders." He left to find a pay phone and a block away, he found one. After attaching his electronic device to the speaker, he placed his call.

"Commander Cummings office. Constable Browne speaking." A young female voice blurted out hurriedly.

"Commander Cummings, please,"

"One moment, sir." The voice said again hurriedly.

"Cummings here."

"Sir, this is Geoffrey. Can your new secretary speak just a wee bit slower? Or is she a temporary secretary?"

"Yes, only temporary. I've lost more phone calls because of her, but she does mean well. I'm transferring another Constable into headquarters. It's someone that I've worked with in the past. Because of our recent troubles, we thoroughly screened all of our employees; even the Metro Police did the same. It helped us clean house quite effectively, so I don't believe there will be any more problems."

"That's good to hear, sir. By the way, the Inspector sends his best regards. It was too bad that you couldn't see his cast. I believe that it will be quite a while before he loses his temper again.

Cummings had a hearty laugh over that. "I imagine that it will be. Well, now that the pleasantries are complete, I'll tell you why I needed you to call. I know that you've been very curious about what happened after you sent those two SAS chaps to me. Well, they were very helpful.

They followed Welsley to a rundown hotel near the docks. After securing the area, the young Captain went in and persuaded the clerk to tell him the room number. He called Leftenant Smythe in, and the two of them went up to the third floor and smashed the door to pieces. They caught both men flat footed. There was a small bit of confusion when Smythe got carried away and let down his guard allowing the other man ... oh, did I tell you about the other man ... of course I didn't; how silly of me.

He was an IRA bomber by the name of Liam Mahr. It seems that the dastardly gentleman had a weapon on him, and he attempted to use it on our two friends. George took immediate action and shot him.

He only wounded him; I know, it had to be on purpose, but he won't talk about it. Regardless, after the Hunting Team arrived, the weapon was retrieved. It, and this is the reason why we did not release any information on this arrest, was a Stechkin 9-millimeter APS." There was a low whistle on the other end of the line.

"Yes, I thought that you would appreciate that bit of news. As we both know that weapon used to be given to senior Soviet field officers. Of course, we had to test fire it and compare the markings on the shell casing to our case load of shootings involving nine-millimeter. We were unable to come up with any matches, but these things do take time; it's not like the flicks. There was something strange about it though; it was almost new. Most of those people's weapons are nicked or the bluing worn in different places in a very short time. This weapon was in excellent condition. One of the lads in the lab believes that it has been out of the original packaging for less than a month because of its condition.

And that's the reason why you, and the Americans, had to wait for the news of the arrest. In fact, we kept it from the press until yesterday. We released the news and let them take their pictures. It was also let known, by some cowardly senior source you understand, that he was being treated like royalty. There was also the promise that if he continued to cooperate, we would help him out in court, if possible."

"Sir, that's a bit of a dirty trick. Why, his people are going to think that he talked." George said knowingly. "Oh, what about George and Harry? They weren't punished for that little mistake, will they?"

"No, they have not been punished. But don't be surprised if you see their names appear on promotion lists much sooner than expected. They also received a medal and a thirty day leave to see their families; you know they earned it."

"Along with the thanks of a grateful country, right? I am in the wrong line of work. This sort of thing doesn't happen to us poor blokes in the civil services, you know."

"Ah, Geoffrey; into each life a little rain must fall. Be grateful that you are kept on in your current position and not out on the street," Cummings added jokingly. "Now for the rest of the news. Because of the informant being found and taken out of the game, you will no longer report to or through Ambassador Ambrose. All of your orders from me or my superiors will go through the FBI. This will help avoid any confusion with people from two different organizations working together. Another reason is courtesy. Next, the fingerprints of the careless killer have arrived and are being searched; we should have something in the next few days. It will take that long because photostatic copies of them are being forwarded to INTERPOL and the Royal Ulster Constabulary. As soon as we get a hit, you three will know.

We'll send pictures of him to Washington so that they can do an identikit on him to see if he matches any of your robbers. I doubt that they are from Ireland and in the U.S. illegally, but we must cover all of the bases. If you have anything to pass on to me, you are to contact me immediately; you have both my numbers.

"That's it from here" Cummings finished. "You take good care of the Inspector for me."

"Will do, sir. Goodbye." Geoffrey took the device off of the phone and hung up. He left the pay phone and returned to his room, where Sam and Ulnar had retreated to while he made his call. He gave them all of the news that he had received. When he was finished, Ulnar spoke up.

I remember that name, Liam Mahr. A nasty bit of business, that. And I would bet that the man who tried his best to murder me is known to Mahr." He fell silent. Then, "Well, this calls for a celebration. Dinner is on me." That caused a minor riot as Geoff and Sam raced to get cleaned up and changed. A free meal from Ulnar Loop was not to be scoffed at.

Two days later their busman's holiday ended with a phone call. Geoff answered the phone. "Hello? Geoffrey Cambridge here."

"This is Bill Williams the SAC at the Boston Field Office. May I speak to Samantha please."

Geoff called her to the phone. "Agent Adams speaking. Yes, Bill. There was? Just a minute let me get a pen and paper. All right; where and when. Sommerset... the Third Trust Bank of Sommerset. Is that the first one or the second one that they hit. Okay. When ... today. Got it. Thanks". She turned and faced her partners, "That was Bill at the bureau. They just repeated themselves by hitting the branch of the Third Trust Bank of Sommerset that they hit the very first time. We need to go down there; they don't have a print person in that town. Inspector", she added," You are about to earn a little pay."

"Back on our heads, coffee break's over." Added Mr. Cambridge.

CHAPTER SIX

The drive out of Boston and to the bedroom community of Sommerset, Massachusetts was made in silence. Geoffrey and Samantha, because of the news that the robbers may be starting to repeat all of their jobs; then again, they might not And Ulnar, because he had just taken a pill to help subdue the pain of the healing arm. Thirty-five minutes after they left the hotel, they arrived outside the twice robbed bank. "Who's in charge here," Samantha asked while flashing her credentials. The officer at the door to the bank pointed his thumb over his shoulder while he tried to pose for the newspaper cameras. "Over by the bank manager's desk." He said, not paying a bit of attention to them.

With Samantha in the lead and the two men in her wake, they walked over to a captain of the local police force. She showed her badge again. He glanced at it and continued to speak to a distraught female bank manager. "So, what'd he looked like, tall, small, what?" he asked in a rude voice.

"I ... really can't remember, sir. It was all ... so ... confusing. All I really did get a good look at was their guns."

"Uh huh, uh huh." He said, writing it down. "Anything else?"

"No, that was all; I'm sorry," she said, near tears.

Samantha stepped in front of the captain; she put her badge directly in front of his face and said, 'Excuse me, captain, but we have been sent here by my superiors to get any information that we can to help catch these people. What can you tell me, sir?"

He looked at her as if she was some new type of plant life. Finally, he said, "Four men, all wearing hats, sunglasses, and raincoats, or overcoats, walked in carrying shotguns. They yelled for everyone except the tellers to hit the floor. Then they ordered the tellers to hand over all of the money. Apparently, one of the tellers was too slow, or he thought she was going to try and put a dye packet in the bag; anyways, he jumped the counter and pushed her out of the way."

"Did he jump over with both hands empty or just one?" She asked him.

"I don't know. What difference does it make, anyhow?"

"What about the film in the cameras? Have they been checked yet?"

"Not yet. But there's no hurry; it's not going anywhere."

Sam gave up. She got with Geoffrey and Ulnar who were watching this exercise in futility. She went over to where it appeared that the tellers were standing. "Who was the unfortunate teller to be in the way of the robber? Was it you?" She asked a short, middle-aged woman who was holding a cold compress to her head. She was trying to stop the bleeding but was failing.

"Yes…. It… it… was, I… I…, just don't understand why he had to push me? If I was in the way, all he had to do was tell me. I didn't even see him until he jumped the counter, and then it was too late."

"Has an ambulance been sent for?" Sam asked.

The teller said yes, one had been sent for. One of her coworkers sent for it, she told them. "I suppose I wasn't getting the money out fast enough. I just started working here last Monday. He didn't have to push me," she said again.

'Where were you working when this happened," Samantha asked gently.

''Right over there," she pointed with her free hand. "Third window from the left. You know those police asked me what they were wearing, and I couldn't remember. All I saw at first was the gun. But I remember now, he wasn't wearing any gloves. I thought that bank robbers always wore gloves. So, they wouldn't leave prints; at least that's what they do on television. Strange."

Sam looked at Geoffrey and Ulnar. Geoff read her mind and immediately walked over to the counter where the teller worked. He asked the captain, who was standing in front of it and still talking to the bank manager, to move. He didn't. Geoffrey Cambridge moved him--with no apologies. Samantha went out to the car and got her fingerprint processing kit that she had been carrying around since they had left D.C. When she returned, she went right over to where the robber jumped the counter. She took out a small clear plastic container along with a small wand that had a magnet inside at one end. The powder inside the container was black with silver specks scattered throughout. This was her own mixture of two magnetic powders, black and silver.

She uncapped the container and put the magnetized end of the wand inside. When she withdrew it there was a small amount of powder attached to it. Then she set the container down, out of her way. She held the magna wand over a small area, and then in a very light circular motion Samantha started to process the surface. She allowed the powder to barely touch the counter. She kept doing this, adding powder when needed, until the entire counter area where the robber climbed over had been processed.

Sam dumped the unused portion of powder back into the container. Then she took her magna wand and went back over the area picking up any stray magnetic powder that had not stuck to any of the fats and oils that were deposited by people touching the counter surface. Carefully, she checked the latent print impressions that had been made visible by the powder to make sure that they were brought out as best as possible without erasing them. This would have happened if Sam had tried to add more manga powder than the fats and oils could absorb.

Satisfied with the results, she asked Ulnar, who was watching her procedure, to get her camera out of the kit. Samantha wanted to take three or four photographs of each of the latent impressions before she did anything else to them. This would ensure that, if there was something with sufficient ridge detail, she would have a latent print that was good enough to compare against known inked prints; even if the impressions lost some of their detail when they were lifted because of the slightly textured surface of the counter.

While she got her camera ready to take the pictures, she said to Geoff, "Mr. Cambridge, would you mind calling the Boston office, and see if they are going to send the agents down here soon?" She gestured to the local police officers. "I believe that they are needed here as soon as possible; if not sooner. Please tell them that I've lifted some prints; one of which might belong to one of the robbers." George left to carry out the request.

"Is there anything that I can do to help?" asked the Inspector. "I feel like I have just dressed up with nowhere to go."

"Yes, sir, you can get some 2x4 inch and a couple of 4x4 inch lifts from my kit. I'll need them as soon as I finish taking my pictures." When she had finished about ten minutes later, he handed them to her.

She took one of the 2x4 lifts and peeled the cellophane from the sticky side. Next, she very carefully took the lift and bent it into a U shape between the thumb and forefinger of the left hand and set the bottom of that U onto one of the groups of partial fingerprints that would fit onto it. She very carefully started to let one side of the U down while rubbing it onto the latent impressions on the counter briskly with her right index finger. When that side was all the way down, she repeated the procedure with the other half of the lift. Then she took a hold of the end of the lift that had a tab on it and in one smooth motion, peeled it off of the counter. She turned around to her kit to get a lift card, but Ulnar already had one in his hand. She set the card down onto another part of the counter and repeated the procedure for lifting so that the lift would be firmly in place on the card. She kept doing this until all of the latent impressions were on cards.

The last step was to thoroughly fill out all of the cards with the correct information, such as time and date, her initials, where the prints were lifted from, etc. She had one of the tellers who was watching her, also initial each card. The case number would have to wait until later, when she could get it from the agents. By the time that she was finished, Geoffrey had returned from his errand.

"That was something to see," he said, referring to her work with the latent. "I had forgotten how much work went into the processing and preservation of latent print evidence. It's been what, ten years since I've had anything to do with that sort of work. In fact, it was in your class, Inspector. Remember?" he asked, reminding Ulnar of the class that they had briefly discussed at the airport a couple of weeks ago.

"Agent Adams, I am quite impressed; you have obviously done your homework very well." Ulnar said. "I wish that people could understand how much work goes into something that, by news accounts, should be very simple. Yet, in fact, it is probably one of the most difficult things to do in the Science of Fingerprints."

"Yes, Inspector. It was once described to me as being like lifting a latent off of an untreated egg. Without proper planning ahead of time, a person can break that egg rather than process a print off of it. During the class that I took in latents, a three hour one to show the basics, I was shown that regardless how hard you try, you cannot do anything without planning ahead."

"I like the egg. Where did you see that?"

"At a small police department in the south. The Latent Examiner giving the class used the egg to show how delicate latent impressions are and how, without proper planning, you can lose your evidence easily; even before you start. The egg was very graphic."

"Hmm... I see. I like that. When I get back to England, I think I'll use that as a visual aid in teaching a class on how to process latent evidence by using powder. This would be open to constables from the Yard and Metro London police. It should get the point across quite well. Thank you for sharing that with me, Samantha. By the way, may I take a look at your lifts?"

She handed the lift cards over to him. "Well, some of the latent impressions may be in question because of the surface of the counter; however, without a magnifying glass I can't say for sure. But I think that your photographs might do the trick. The latents looked quite good on the surface of the counter." Samantha Adams beamed and blushed at the same time, at this compliment coming from the foremost authority in the Science of Fingerprints. "As I said earlier, if only more people only knew how much work goes into something that looks so easy and so simple. Oh, well," he sighed as he handed the latent lift cards back to her. She put them in a special envelope that was in her kit.

She filled the envelope out with the proper information. Then she signed and dated it. When the other agents arrived fifteen minutes later, Samantha walked over to the agent in charge of the investigation and signed the latent print evidence over to him.

"Thank you, Agent Adams. Bill Williams told me to look for you and your charges, so that you could fill me in on what I need to get in the way of information from the victims."

"Everything," she answered. "You saw the television idol at the bank entrance when you came in, didn't you?" she asked, nodding her head in the direction of the front door. "Well, it's not any better in here. That Captain over there was the only other officer on the scene when we got here."

"Is it that bad?" asked Christopher Cross, the lead agent.

"Worse; we even have an injured civilian over there. He didn't call for medical treatment or an ambulance, a co-worker did. Personally," she said in a loud whisper, "I wouldn't hire him to clean the trash bins at a law enforcement's training facility."

"Well, that gives me a good idea on where to start. At the very beginning." He spoke to his assistant, Antoine Martin.

"Antoine, get those two officers, the one at the door and the useless captain, relieved and out of the way. Then, let's get a proper crime scene set up. When the agent is at the door, have him start a list of law enforcement people at the scene, including us. I'll have Johns get the names of the other people in here before he interviews them; that way, one person will have all the names. It'll probably save us a lot of headaches later. After you take care of that, babysit the injured teller. She's our best chance for information on that one bandit."

After Chris had gotten Agent Johns started on his duties of recording and then interviewing the people who were inside the bank at the time of the robbery, he crossed the lobby to the agent from the lab. He signed Sam's evidence over to him and instructed him on where she found the latent prints. This way he would not waste time on that section of the counter. On his way to the Inspector and his friends to tell them what was being done, he passed out gloves to the other agents so that they would not contaminate the scene. Actually, it was only Geoffrey who did not grasp everything that he saw. Ulnar had not only done crime scenes while he worked at Scotland Yard, but he had taught the subject to new lab people. Samantha needed that training as part of her job as an FBI Agent. They could see that everything was being done, so they put their hands in their pockets and walked over to where the two police officers were sullenly sitting, safely out of the way.

Agent Cross began to assist Agent Johns in the process of interviewing and information gathering.

Agent Martin, having discharged his other duties, first checked on the status of the ambulance, and then walked over to the injured teller. Even from this distance, he could tell that she was not doing well. "Ma'am?" He asked as he came to her.

She looked up into his large brown eyes and caring face. "Yes?" she said in a weak and strained voice. "Who are you?"

"My name is Antoine Martin," he said, showing her and her friend his badge and credentials. He went over and got the injured woman a chair. When she was seated, he went on in his soft voice. "I just checked if the ambulance will be here any minute now. What I would like to do is accompany you to the hospital and make sure that you get the treatment that you need."

"You'll also need to ask me some questions about what happened, won't you?"

"Yes, ma' a ... "

"My name is Ruth, Ruth Yankovitch."

"Yes, Mrs. Yankovitch. That's exactly what I need to do," he said with a warm smile. "But our first concern is for your health. Let's get you to the hospital ER first, and then we'll talk about what happened when those men came in. Fair enough?"

"Yes, it is. Mr ... "

"Martin.."

"Mr. Martin. Can my friend come along?" She asked, at the same time touching the arm of the woman next to her.

"Certainly. I think that would be a very good idea." Just then he saw the flashing lights of the ambulance as it pulled up outside of the bank. "Here's your ride."

After the ambulance attendants had fought their way through the mass of media personnel, they came into the bank lobby and checked out Mrs. Yankovitch. "You two ladies ride in the ambulance, and I'll take my car and meet you there." He made sure that the injured teller was properly taken care of, got into his vehicle, and drove to the hospital. He met them at the admissions office.

The two ladies looked lost among the other bandaged, bleeding victims of that day's crimes and accidents. "Have you been helped yet?" He asked Mrs. Yankovitch.

Before Ruth could answer, her friend sharply spoke up, "No! She hasn't!" She looked at Agent Martin and saw the honest concern on his face. "I'm sorry, but no, no one has asked anything. And I'm concerned about her wound. I know head injuries bleed a lot, but this is the third damp cloth she's had, and it's still soaking through. The paramedics even put a bandage on it. Still not much help ... " She ran out of breath. Mrs. Yankovitch stared helplessly at Antoine.

"I see." Is all that he said. But usually more is done when little is said. This was to be a case in point. He walked over to the admitting desk and stood silently there until someone looked up.

"Yes? May I help you?"

"Yes, you may. Why hasn't that woman over there been, at the very least, wheeled back to one of your cubicles?" he asked, pointing at Ruth. "I have been here for only a few minutes, but in that time, I've seen people with less wrong with them get help first.

Now, ma'am, I am not here to tell you about your job; however, it seems to me that when a patient comes in on an ambulance, then it may be fairly serious. Besides the obvious head wound, this woman is a victim of a bank robbery in which the injury occurred. On top of that," he went on in the same, very quiet voice, "She had to wait for at least a half hour for it to get to her. If I were her, after this is all over, I would contact a good lawyer to make sure that this shoddy treatment never happens again." Finished, he stood silently looking at the admissions clerk.

The clerk suddenly became very busy by getting an orderly to wheel Ruth back to a treatment room, contacting a doctor, and filling out the correct admission forms. About fifteen minutes later, Ruth was having her head x-rayed to make sure that there was no concussion. Forty-five minutes after that, she had a local injected into the sight of the head wound and was being stitched up. Agent Martin kept his promise; he never left her side. While she was having her head sewed up, she reached out her hand to him. He held gently onto her hand until she was taken up to a room. It had been decided that, although she had not suffered a concussion, she should remain overnight for observation. No one ever found out that Antoine Martin had suggested that this would be a good idea.

As she was being taken to her room, he went out to inform her friend of what had been done. He told her that if she waited for a short time, she would be able to go to Ruth's room and see her for a few minutes. After her friend from the bank left, he would go to see her and start to slowly, and carefully, get her story on what had happened at the bank. More importantly, though, he would also get a description of the robber. He knew that this would take a while, but he was a patient man. That night there would be a guard outside her room; the bad guys would know that she may have gotten a good look at them, and the FBI did not want to lose her.

Agent Martin softly knocked on the door to her room and then peeked around the corner of the door. ''Hello, Mrs. Yankovitch,'' he said cheerily. "And how is the hospital's favorite patient doing?"

She quickly arranged her bedclothes and said, 'Please, come in. Excuse the way I look, but no one has ... you know. I ...I'm ... well this is a first for me. I really don't know how to act ...I know that it sounds silly, but..."

"That's alright. Please don't worry about it, Mrs. Yankovitch. You're doing okay, and you look just fine. How are you feeling?"

"Much better, thank you. The head is a little sore, but other than that, fine."

''Here," he continued, holding out his left hand which, up until now, was hidden behind his back, "I hope you like flowers. I thought that they might cheer you up."

"Oh, my. I do love flowers. And they are just perfect. Could you please put them in some water?" He went about the room and got something to put the flowers into and then got some water. When he was finished, he put them on the night stand next to her bed. He brought a chair up to the bed and sat down.

"Mrs. Yankovi ... " he started.

''Please, call me Ruth. All of my friends do, and I would like to think of you as a friend; especially after what happened."

"I would consider it an honor to be your friend, Ruth. Thank you. Would you mind if I ask you a few questions about this afternoon?"

"No, I don't mind. I knew that you would have to start doing that sooner or later."

"Look, Ruth, if it gets difficult at any time for you, we'll stop. I'm not here to pressure you, but, since you are the only witness to get a look at one of the robbers close up, we need to start now."

She reached out her right hand to him and touched his hand, again, he gently held it. This seemed to give her assurance as well as confidence that all would be right with the world. "I understand.

Early this afternoon, right after lunch, when the bank was fairly empty of customers, these four men with those ridiculous hats, and those sunglasses. On a cloudy day yet. Who do they think they were fooling." She sighed. "I'm sorry, but I was scared, terribly scared. These things happen to other people, not me. Right now, though, I'm beginning to get mad. If only my husband could've lived long enough to see this. Me, mad," she laughed a small laugh. But it was an improvement.

"My husband died two years ago. I had just started working in the bank to have something to do. Many of my friends have their gardening and their clubs. But, well, that's never been for me. And, until recently, I didn't want to get involved with anything. So, I started to work. It looked like fun, and I would meet new people; maybe make some new friends. You know, like the one from the bank." Antoine sat through this disconnected talk. He had interviewed many people after this sort of crime, and it was a normal reaction. Considering her age, personal life, and injury during an armed robbery, she was doing quite well.

"Anyway, these four men came into the bank with those awful costumes."

"Costumes?"

"Well, as I said, those hats, sunglasses, and coats. They looked like gangsters from some B movie. They waved those shotguns around, telling everyone to lie down on the floor; well, everyone except the tellers. We were to take the money out of the cash drawers and fill the sacks that were placed in front of us. But..."

"But what, Ruth? Was there something unusual ... well ... other than their dress?"

"Their language. Oh, I don't mean that they cursed or anything, but it was the way they talked. Their accents. I really didn't give it any thought until now. Isn't that funny?" She laid there, silent. In thought Antoine waited a moment or two.

"What's funny, Ruth? What was funny about their accents?"

"Hmm? Oh. Yes, their accents. Very Irish. But a different Irish accent than those people have who try to pretend that they're from Ireland. It was, as my grandson would say, 'the real deal'. You're probably wondering how I know? Well, it's very simple. I was born Ruth McLeod and raised in a very Irish neighborhood. Many of the relatives, both mine and my friends, were straight from the auld sod." Again, silence.

"You know, the more I think about it, the more I'm sure of it. They are either just over here on a boat, or..."

"Or their being here is not kosher." Agent Martin finished.

Ruth nodded her head.

"Hmm. That's an excellent point, Ruth. My superiors will be very interested in that observation. Is there anything else about them that you remember?"

"Well, did I mention that they didn't wear gloves? I think I mentioned it to somebody; although, I don't remember who right now. But I remember thinking how strange that was. Bank robbers without gloves. Why, it's almost like they either didn't care about being caught, or they didn't think ... oh, I don't know what to think." She spoke. Suddenly, she grabbed her head; her face showing pain.

Antoine held her hand and with his other, he pressed the call button. A nurse appeared and he said that he believed that she would need something for the pain. The nurse shooed him out of the room and summoned her doctor. They gave her a sedative, and the doctor made the decision that if Ruth's pain should continue, he was going to order an MRI to make sure that there was no damage to the brain.

When they were finished with her, Agent Martin came back into the room. "I understand that you've been given some more medication. I'll come back tomorrow and check on you. If you're feeling up to it then, we'll continue with our talk. And don't worry. There'll be nurses checking on you throughout the night to make sure that everything is fine. Okay?"

''Yes, that will be fine, Antoine." She said drowsily. In a few minutes the sedative had taken effect, and she was sound asleep. He left and placed a call to the office for another agent to guard the door to her room. When the relief was in place, he went back to the office to make a complete report on what he had learned so far. This included her observations on the possible nationality of the robbers. Later, when notes were compared by the FBI, Scotland Yard, and the Inspector and his friends, it was going be quite obvious that an opening to the case was about to be made.

The next day, as Antoine was completing his report, the second person to make the leap in logic as far as the nationality of the suspects was concerned, was having a cup of tea with the Inspector. "I know that I didn't have time to thank you yesterday, Inspector. But I will now. Thank you."

''Why, Geoffrey, whatever for?'

"The way you explained what was going on at the bank, without making me feel like a fool. I was totally out of my element. Having worked in the areas that I have at the Yard, I've lost all touch with ordinary crimes."

''Don't be so hard on yourself, Geoff When it comes to dealing with terrorists or mad bombers, you would be the first person I would call. Granted, you didn't understand much yesterday; however, many people wouldn't. You have those talents that are yours alone. So, there is no reason for any type of apology or thanks."

"I wonder if Sam has come up with anything new. She's been on the phone for quite a while," said Geoffrey, going onto another subject.

"As I understand it, she is making a complete report to the local office ... umm ... to that Bill Williams chap. By the way Mr. Cambridge," he said with a twinkle in his eye, 'You're not becoming infatuated with Agent Adams. Are you?"

"I'm sorry Inspector, but I don't know what you're talking about. I have a great deal of respect for her as an FBI Agent. But anything else is ... not so."

"That's fine Geoff I was just making an observation, that's all. Nothing personal." He finished with a look on his face that did not reflect what he had just said. "Let's go up to the room and see what she has to say for herself Perhaps it is more news on the robbery, or maybe she's heard something on that poor woman at the bank." They had the check put on their room bill, along with a tip, and left.

While they went back to their room, and then into Agent Adam's room, people in another, older hotel, which was a few blocks away, were also discussing the robbery.

"Alright Sean, once again. Why did you make that careless move at that Sommerset bank? That woman was moving as fast as the others. But no. You had to jump over the counter and push her. Granted they don't know who we are, but don't forget we don't need to wear gloves. You may have left a smudged print, but we don't want to give them anything," said the man with the scared hand, Martin Dunn.

"Alright, Martin, I fouled up. It looked like she was going to put a dye packet, or whatever the Americans call it, in with the money," replied Sean Flaherty.

"That might be so, Sean, but if I find out that you've endangered our movement by your carelessness, I will personally punish you," Martin said in a dangerous voice. "You had better be extra careful from now on, lad." He said in a more menacing, tone.

At that moment, the cellular phone rang on the cheap, cracked hotel table. Martin picked it up and flipped it open. "Yes." He said.

The voice on the other end said, 'You guys were really sloppy at the bank. A lot of people have made sure that you guys could do these heists without a problem of being caught. The bosses didn't have to help ya, ya remember. Ya could've been on yer own, trying to do these jobs. I don't think ya'd of gotten as far as ya have without that help."

"Yes, that's right, but what about all of the money that you and your people have received? You have received exactly half of the money from each of the robberies. So, we have paid our dues, so to speak."

"Maybe, maybe not. The bosses will decide that. Like I said, they ain't really happy about how this job went down. Real careless. I hear that a teller got hurt an' she's in the hospital. Ya better pray that nothin happens to her. Yer help could disappear real fast; ya know what I'm sayin, sport?"

"Yes, I do." Martin replied. "But, what about our next job? Will it be large enough that we can finally be finished with this line of work?"

"We'll get t' that in a minute. Right now, I need t' tell ya about the source of infermation that we used t' tell us where that Inspector fella could be found. Seems that the source and our Irish guy he told this stuff ta, were caught. Yer guy got hit with a slug, but he's goin t' be okay. Of course, the cops have em both, and yer guy could spill the beans to em. Nobody keeps quiet no more. But, ya know that already. I hope that he don't know much about yer operation, er else yer dead meat," the voice added, taking pleasure in upsetting the leader of the robbers.

"Also, the bosses wanted me t' tell ya that yer on thin ice. First off, ya blew the job of icin that inspector type guy. Then ya messed up with that one bank; huh, came away with nuthin. They wern't happy with that at all, but this last job ... oh yeah, .. you guys really messed up. Ya got real careless this time," the voice said, repeating himself, because he knew that this would definitely upset Martin.

"Yes, you said that already." Martin sighed. "And I understand what you are saying, but we need to talk about this last robbery. Ahem; so that we may get back to Ireland and continue to fight for freedom against the Engli ... "

"Hey, fancy talker. Lemme finish wit this. The bosses said that if the old dame croaks, then ya won't get no more help. That means if yer stuck here tryin t' get outta the country, everything'll shut down. You'll have t' find yer own way out. Ya won't get no help from us."

"Anything else?" Martin asked, gritting his teeth. He had had just about all that he could stomach from the voice. "Or are you finally going to tell us how to accomplish our last job."

"Yeah, the last job. But yer goin t' wait a week or so before ya do it. The bosses say that this'll give things a chance t' cool down. And like I said, they also wanna see if the teller lives or not." Finally, the voice at the other end of the phone started to inform Martin of the plan for the last robbery. At least there were parts of it that he and his lads had done before.

For Martin's part, he controlled himself well. He admitted that the voice was correct on their failures, but it still hurt. He desperately wanted to leave this country and get back to Ireland. Because he was a professional in the terrorist community and not at bank robbery, he listened very carefully to the voice on the phone as it described in extreme detail the workings of this, the final heist.

As those plans were being explained, Samantha was on the phone with Bill Williams, the Special Agent in Charge of the local field office. Geoffrey and Ulnar had returned to their room and waited there for her to finish the conversation.

"So that's it Sam. According to Special Assistant Director Noma, they have matched the prints of the careless crook that tried to take out the Inspector with a set on file with the Royal Ulster Constabulary. It seems that they are identical with a certain John Flynn. From what they say, he's a real piece of work. He's been a suspect in a number of bombings of department stores in which women and children have been the main target. He's also been involved with several kidnapping of political targets and rivals from the other so called revolutionary groups.

They've sent his picture over along with a photostatic copy of the prints. Right now, headquarters is going to enter the photo into the special software program of theirs and see if it comes close to any of the composite drawings from the earlier robberies. With any luck we can make his life very interesting with the extra charges. He can figure to spend the rest of his natural life in a federal, gray bar hotel. If we turn him over to the British for those murders, then he may not even live out his sentence. You've heard that even English convicts, for the most part, are very loyal to the crown, and those who bomb innocent women and children are not going to get a very nice welcome."

"Yes, I have," replied Samantha Adams. "What other news do you have for me. You did mention some other fingerprint cards that are on the way over here, too. Oh, and those palmprints. Will we be able to have anything from the RUC to compare against those palms from the last robbery?"

"Yes, we will. It seems that the Irish police take their fingerprinting duties very seriously. When these low-lives get arrested on any charge at all, the law enforcement agencies, if they get a break on any of the more serious crimes that the slimes are suspected of, take major case prints on them. Whole rolled fingers, tips of the fingers, and of course, the palms themselves. That's in addition to the rolled end joints of the fingers. So, we will have some comparison to make if we get anymore breaks on these cases. Pictures, of course, are also being sent. That will be one busy computer program for awhile."

"So, from what you've told me, the teller was right about them not being from here. That was a good job that your Agent Martin did working with her. By the way, how's she coming along? Even during that brief time that I had talked to her, I found her to be a very competent witness. Very observant."

"I don't know yet. The doctors are supposed to do an MRI on her later today. Seems that she's developed some severe headaches not long after she was admitted. I'm going to send Antoine back to her before she has the scan to be there for support. Afterwards we'll see if he can get that description of the one that jumped the counter."

"That's great, Bill. I'll pass the word on to the Inspector and Mr. Cambridge. I know they'll be glad to hear that these leads have been developed. Take care of yourself."

"Thanks, Sam. You do the same. Goodbye."

She hung up the phone and walked into the next room after knocking on the connecting door. "Is everyone decent?"

"Unfortunately, yes," said the Inspector. "Well, now. What did Agent Williams have to tell you?"

"Quite a bit," she said. She found that when she looked at the two men, they had very pale complexions. "You know you two have been cooped up indoors for far too long. Why haven't you been out for any exercise lately? Keep this up and you'll both vegetate or get sick. You've got to leave the hotel and see some of the sights."

"Well, we would," replied Geoff. "Except that the Inspector has a problem with the local weather."

Ulnar spoke up. "Dear lady," he said exaggerating his tone of voice, "How can anyone possibly survive in that moist oven you call weather? Why, it's simply awwwful. I thought that in the northern part of your country it would be somewhat cooler."

"Normally, it is." Samantha replied. "However, during the height of summer, especially in some cities, it can be very hot and humid. Not to worry, though. According to the local weather people, we're in for some bad storms either late tonight or early tomorrow. They're supposed to blow through here quite rapidly. After they've passed by then it will cool down to the high seventies. Then you will not have any excuse to get some exercise. Besides, sir, I would feel terrible if anything were to happen to you if you don't get out. And we can keep an easy eye on you with that bright cast."

Ulnar Loop did not reply to the remark of the eyesore that was wrapped around his arm between the elbow and the knuckles of his right hand. Instead, he said, "Thank goodness that it will finally come off later this week. The doctor has said that I am healing quite well for a man of my age."

"I'm glad to hear that, Inspector. Now, are you two ready for some good news."

"Geoffrey Cambridge spoke up. "Definitely".

"It seems that the robbers are from Ireland. The man who tried to kill you, Inspector, has been identified as one John Flynn," she said, referring to her notes. "Apparently, he's a very bad boy, even by terrorist standards. They think that they know who he's running with. The Royal Ulster Constabulary is sending all available major case prints and photos of them to Washington. That reminds me, I'll have them express them up to Boston since the latent impressions are still here."

"Then what the teller had observed was true, or at least partly true," said Ulnar. "But why are they in America, robbing banks?"

"Good question, sir." Said Geoff There was silence. The only sounds were the muffled sounds of the traffic, far below. "And I think I can answer that. Remember that Russian nine-millimeter I said was found on Liam Mahr, and it was like new? Well, at least Sam has heard, that the Russian Mafia is getting bolder. They're selling a lot of military equipment. What with the inflation over there and those few that have jobs, get either low or no pay. People everywhere are selling anything they can lay their hands on. The Soviets used to supply the terrorists, but now they're on their own; even old Fidel can't help. Now, they must purchase all of it, except what is donated to them by some other sick organizations. Drugs used to be a big help, but between our two governments, we've closed many of their supply lines down. They need money, and they need it badly. Guns and explosives are not cheap." He slapped his forehead with his hand. "AHH! I should have seen it. That's why they didn't wear gloves, and why they seemed so clumsy and inept at robbing banks. We had no prints and they were careful not to leave any. At least, not until now.

Another thing, I remember now what I was trying to think of back at Perry Swordes office. Their attire. The lady from the bank was right, bless her soul." The other two looked at Geoffrey Cambridge strangely. "The attire. Don't you see? Even she mentioned that it looked like a costume. That's what I missed. Back when this first started and our messages were coming from the Embassy, Ambassador Ambrose made a comment about how the robbers were seen to be imitating American gangsters. You see? Because of their dress. They look like something out of a B movie ... " he stopped. "Yes, just like your teller said. Wasn't that mentioned in the report, Samantha?"

"The one sent to me from the field office; yes. Yes, it was," she said with understanding coming over her. "How simple; how marvelously simple. Right in front of us all of the time, and we never saw it. Well, sometimes it does take another person's view to make you see the beauty of the trees and not just the forest."

"One thing you both have seemed to have forgotten," Ulnar spoke up. Samantha and Geoffrey turned and looked at him.

"What's that, sir?" Geoff asked.

"Look at all of the robberies they have committed, and they have never been caught. They even know when the best time is to rob as well. The only robbery that failed was in that town ... oh, what is it's name ... " He said in exasperation.

"Wormwood ... Smaller Wormwood; that's it." Samantha said.

"Righto! That's the one! The guards seemed to be extra cautious, because of the other robberies. Yet, at the other banks they acted as if they were surprised. And all of your newspaper and media news kept telling everyone about them. These are terrorists, killers of the defenseless. Not bank robbers. Pushers and murderers, yes. Robbers, no." Ulnar was in his element. Deducing; taking things apart and putting them back together again. Just as he had done with fingerprints and crime scenes when he had worked for Scotland Yard. Pacing back and forth, he continued, "Why were the guards at the other banks so asleep, while at the Smaller Wormwood bank, they weren't? And the guards at the Third Bank of Sommerset, the one that was the first to be held up, they were not even alert this time. The robbers just walked right in and took what they wanted. It has become a very curious thing about these guards."

"Exactly!" Samantha exclaimed. "Who hired the guards; who were they hired from; when were they hired? And," she said raising her hand up with the index finger extended," Who is giving the robbers the ideal times and places to commit these felonies? I don't know if we can do anything about the last question," she said in a quieter voice, "But we might be able to do something about the first one. I'll contact Bill at the field office." She looked at her watch to see if, because of the time, he would be in his office and not at lunch. "Humph." Nearly two P.M.; how time flies. Well, unless he's taking a late lunch, he should be in."

He was in and at his desk. "Samantha, what can I do for you?" He asked when he answered his phone.

"Bill, we've come up with a question. -Has anyone started looking into the situation about the bank guards.?" She went on to explain in detail what the three of them had been discussing. Twenty minutes later she finished. "Well?"

"Let me see." He started to paw through the pile of reports that these robberies had generated. Reports on all of the follow-up questions that come along as new questions arise. Reports that go back over the lists of witnesses and any evidence that they might have missed. And, as in all large cases, it seems that there are even reports on reports. "Ah, here it is.

Yes. It seems that all of the guards, except the ones in the bungled job, were hired from the same rent a cop agency. Mmm, maybe from three to six months before the robberies took place. That agency has since closed down and none of the people who managed it can be reached for any comment. They've just disappeared. We have some of the state agencies who license these businesses looking into their records, and I've got an agent running down anything we can find on it. However, as you yourself know Samantha, we have just so much manpower for all of these robberies, and then we're still looking for the perps who did the jobs. The local cops can look into their individual robberies to help us, well, except for the Sommerset cops.

As a matter of fact, we have the state investigators looking into that sorry lot. They've taken over the small force and are turning up good evidence on some of the other crimes that have happened in that town. Of course, that does not help us with robberies, but anytime you can crush crime in any form, it doesn't matter how the start of it happened. Like I said, though, nothing much yet on the rent a cop situation. I appreciate your input and if you get anything more, please call."

"Okay, thanks, Bill." She hung up the phone.

"What did he say," asked Ulnar.

She explained what she had been told. Then, "But by the sound of his voice and the way he ended the conversation, I don't think that he was all that interested in what we've come up with. In a way I don't blame him; in the same position I might act the same way. He's got just so much manpower, and all of the pressure from all sides to solve these robberies is wearing him down. And, as we all know, this type of thing happens whether we like it or not."

"What about Agent Martin? I wonder if he is at the hospital, yet?" Mused Ulnar.

Sam said, 'I believe so. The teller is supposed to be scanned in approximately thirty minutes, and I understand that he wanted to be there before she was wheeled from her room."

CHAPTER SEVEN

"Agent Martin was at the hospital with Ruth Yankovitch, the injured teller from the bank. She was waiting to be wheeled down to the room where she would be scanned by the MRI. "Thank you for coming, Mr. Martin.

""Remember, Ruth, that's Antoine. And you're welcome. But I wanted to be here to keep you company during this. Besides, I thought that we could relax a little and talk while we waited. Why don't you tell me a little about yourself?" He asked.

"She started by saying that she had been born in 1938. She told about the growing up in an all-Irish neighborhood, her childhood, marriage, and her two sons. When she got to that part, a nurse came in to tell her that it was time. An orderly also entered and helped her onto the gurney. Ruth asked Antoine if he would be going with her, and he told her that no, he couldn't; but he would be waiting for her when she returned. He gave her hand an extra squeeze as she left for the MRI. A nervous smile appeared on her face. It was better than nothing.

"An hour later, Ruth had not come back from the MRI. Agent Martin went to the nurses station to ask about Mrs. Yankovitch. The nurse would not give him any information. Although he had known Ruth Yankovitch for only 24 hours, it seemed that it was much more than that. This sometimes happens when people are deeply caring and not shallow. For the first time in his bureau career, Special Agent Antoine Martin lost his cool, just a little, and pulled out his credentials;

he shoved them in front of the nurse's face; he demanded that he be told where she was, and where she was at this moment. The nurse, taken by surprise with his abrupt conduct, called for a doctor.

"When the doctor appeared, Antoine had cooled down some and apologized to the nurse. He turned to face the doctor and asked what had happened to his friend Mrs. Yankovitch. After all, she had gone down for an MRI, and that was only as a precaution because of her headaches. He also explained that she was an important witness for his agency because she was an eyewitness to the bank robbery. All to no avail. Finally, he went to a pay phone and called Bill Williams, who called Special Assistant Director Melvin A. Noma. The director of the FBI, Charles Dickinson, called the hospital's chief surgeon. He rushed down to the third floor and told the doctor that this woman was a Very Important Person, and he should cooperate in any way that he could.

"The doctor personally took Agent Martin down to the surgical wing. They found Ruth in pre-op. She had already gotten the shot to relax her. But even with that, she was still very nervous and wondering what was happening. No one had really told her; they had only said that she needed emergency surgery. Antoine came into the room and walked over to her. She held out her hand; he took it gently in his. She looked into his eyes and asked what was happening, knowing that he could not and would not lie to her. The doctor had briefed him on the way to pre-op, so he could answer this very important question.

""Ruth ... "he hesitated and tried again. "Ruth. The headaches that you started having yesterday and are still having, are being caused by the injury to your head from the robbery." She looked confused. "I know that it doesn't make much sense, but a few things do. Apparently, there was a very weak artery in your brain. The blow to your temple made it so the artery could not pass blood in a certain section. The blood is gathering there and cannot go any further. It is putting a lot of pressure on your brain, and if it keeps up it will make you pass out. It could very easily kill you if it is not taken care of immediately." They discovered it when you had the MRI. That's why you have been rushed down here for this surgery."

""Am I going to be okay," she asked in her bravest voice. "Will I live?" She asked in a voice that demanded, and yet, was choked with emotion. Tears were rising up in her eyes.

"He looked into the doctor's face; a face that was seeing the beginning of a death. He very quietly said that he did not know. He wasn't the neurosurgeon. Antoine said, "I really can't tell you Ruth. I wish to heaven that I could, but no one knows yet."

"She continued to look up into his honest, caring face, "I understand, Antoine." She said as she gripped his hand even harder. They wheeled her to the operating room.

"He left her briefly so that he could get into some greens. He was going to be in that room with her, no matter what the hospital wanted. A few minutes later he came in with the doctor. Just before she went under from the anesthesia, she saw his face and weakly smiled. He smiled from behind his mask and winked back at her.

"Hours later, in a waiting room, Agent Martin was found sitting and staring at the wall in front of him. The doctor came in; he was exhausted from the surgery. "I'm sorry, but we couldn't save her. It was going fine and then ... the blasted thing just ruptured! We couldn't save her," he repeated in a tired, defeated voice.

"Antoine went over and shook the doctor's hand, telling him that he believed the doctor had done all that he could possibly do. The doctor thanked him, and with a very defeated walk, his head down, he left the waiting room. Antoine went to a pay phone to call the agent on duty. That agent would call Bill Williams and then the two of them would get in touch with the next of kin. This would be her only surviving son who lived in California. The other had been killed in Viet Nam. Antoine, after he helped make these calls, dragged his tired, emotionally drained body, out of the hospital and to the office where he would write up his report. There would not be any description available of the person who helped end her life. There would also be no Ruth Yankovitch.

"The next morning Samantha got a call from Agent Williams telling her what had happened to the eyewitness. Later that day the news of Ruth's death would go out over the news services. Two days later, her son, their relatives, and friends, including FBI Special Agent Antoine Martin, would pay their last respects to her; she would be buried next to her husband.

"The morning of the funeral was overcast and humid; rain was threatening. At the end of the service, when her mortal remains were being lowered into the ground, a tiny section of the clouds parted, and a ray of sunlight burst through to shine down upon the service. At that moment the birds that had been brightly singing stopped. As if to pay respect to a fine person. That same day, a body was found in a dumpster.

"It was taken to the morgue as a John Doe; just one of many for that day. No particular attention was paid at that time to the body; it became just another statistic on the back page of the newspaper. There was not more than a fifteen second piece done on it on the television news. Except, to say that it showed the city was on its way to a record year for homicides.

"With nothing more important to do at this time, Samantha, Geoffrey, and the Inspector went down to the field office to help sort through, and correlate, the reports that were still coming through from the different agencies on the robberies. There was still no new information on who hired the guards for those banks. Whoever it was, had done a thorough job in covering their tracks. As if by magic the bank guards in question had also disappeared.

"A week after the funeral, on his last day in Boston, the Inspector had the flashy pink cast removed. He was given exercises to do so that his wrist and hand could supposedly regain their former strength. When he left the room where it had been removed, Geoffrey Cambridge was waiting for him. "Well sir, do you feel better now that your fashion setting cast is off?" Ulnar did not bother to answer the question. Instead, he turned his head forward and intentionally walked towards the elevators.

"Samantha was waiting for them when they got back to their room. "Well, our hero returns. How's the arm, Inspector?"

""Although it is better than I thought it would be, the hand and wrist are still quite weak. However, the best news is that I can now clean my arm. After all those weeks in a cast, which kept it from being washed, it has built up quite a bit of odor and filth. So! I will repair the bathroom and properly clean myself up."

"After he left, Samantha and Geoffrey sat down at the small table in his room. "Well, he does seem to be in better spirits now that the cast is off.""

""Yes, it would seem that he didn't care for it one bit. Of course, when he did complain, I reminded him that it was his own fault because of the tantrum that he threw in the hospital back in New York City. He forgot that people who don't know him ... well ... they're not going to excuse his attitude just because he's different, or important. Also, here in America some people have different types of humor when it comes to dealing with people like him." He sighed, "Well, it's all water under the bridge, now.""

"Ulnar walked out of his bedroom looking much more refreshed. "Ahh, that feels better. You know, we were talking about the guards at the banks and how the robbers knew everything. And, how unpredictable they are. So, while I was freshening up, I started to think about these crimes. The scum has only missed one bank. Do you think that there is the possibility that they may go back and straighten out their record?"

"Samantha and Geoffrey looked at him. "Hmm, there might be something to that thought, Inspector," she said. "In fact, I've had a nagging feeling in the back of my mind concerning that very subject. They've been so unpredictable, and why not? There's certainly nothing to stop them. Why, even their pace picked up until that last heist. They're apparently laying low for some reason."

""That may have been due to the injury to Mrs. Yankovitch. They may have decided to wait until they found out what would happen to her. Their leader may not have wanted to keep anyone around who was a danger to the brigade. A stupid move like the one that was pulled off in the bank, normally makes a person in a terrorist gang disappear for good. Once they found out whether she lived or died, then they would make their move." Geoffrey added.

""'By now, they would know what happened to Mrs. Yankovitch. But do you really think they would get rid of the one who was the cause of it all.?" Samantha asked.

""'Knowing them the way I do? Yes! Yes, they would; in a heartbeat."

""'And" Ulnar added, "After they made their move, which was to get rid the person that caused the problem, they are going to do another job."

""'Yes sir, they are. And that will be the bank in Smaller Wormwood. I've got a very good feeling that these men will finish what they started. Or the people who are telling them what to do are finishing it. Either way, I believe that they are going to outsmart themselves." Concluded Geoff.

""'Then I'll call Bill and let him know what we've come up with. Again, maybe he and his men have already come to the same conclusion. However, we'll never know until we discuss it with him." She went over to her cellular phone and placed the call. It was picked up on the first ring.

""'Bill, this is Samantha. We've been discussing the robbers and came up with two ideas. First, we strongly believe that they may have gotten rid of the robber who injured the teller, and secondly, that they may go for the bank that they bungled."

""'I was about to call you people to let you know that a body was discovered on the day of her funeral. The Boston cops just told us about it. It seems that there was a John Doe at the morgue; of course, there's nothing strange about that. However, all the normal points of identity were gone. Again, this is not uncommon in a city that has so many of the bent nosed types. But this one also had had a great deal of dentistry done on his teeth. Work that could only have been done in the Eastern Block countries. That was why they called us in on it."

""Great. Do you have any of the major case prints from Ireland yet, so that you can have a comparison made on the post-mortem palm prints and the ones from the bank?"

""No. Nothing has arrived yet from headquarters. I've given them a call to see when the pictures, composites, and prints could be sent, but Mr. Noma didn't know. He's going to call as soon as he finds out. When he does, we're going to have the Senior Latent Examiner over at the P.D. compare those prints to the ones from the bank. At least the ones that are left."

""'Left?"

""Yeah. We were lucky that there had been very few people in the bank that day. All of them were known to the employees because they're regulars .. And in some cases, neighbors. We were able to get them down here for elimination prints. We also printed the employees and those two dippy officers from the Sommerset P.D.

"Turns out that the Captain's prints were identical with some of the fingertips on the counter. Apparently, he had been drumming his fingers where the perp jumped the counter. By the way, he's on unpaid leave and has been told that he better find another line of work. Seems that this isn't the first crime scene he's damaged. The Commonwealth will file criminal charges if he doesn't quit. The movie 'idle' had his fifteen minutes of shame from the scene and has been fired. I don't think that the Sommerset city council is going to give either one a job recommendation. But, from what I've heard, they're going to push the forensic sciences and hire competent people in those fields.

"Let's see ... a few of the other latent impressions that were good belonged to the customers. According to the Latent Examiner's report" ... there was a rustling sound of papers that could be heard, "There were eight impressions that did not have enough ridge detail for comparison purposes, excuse me, couldn't be compared due to the lack of 'points'. The palmprint is still good, but the other thirteen prints, mostly tips of fingers and edges of palms, belonged to the people I mentioned."

""Then, so far, so good. I hope your luck holds, Bill. The other reason I called was to let you know that we're heading for Smaller Wormwood. Mr. Cambridge said that they would probably dispose of the guy who injured the teller. Now he thinks that they may complete the job that they fouled up. I happen to agree."

""I thought of that, too. So, I called up the police department there and told them the same thing. They've informed the bank and have got increased patrols in the area. There's nothing else that we can do officially. If you can, do so. And tell us of anything that you learn.

""I will, Bill. Bye." Agent Adams closed up the phone. She returned through the connecting door to Geoff's room and told them about the prints and that the police in Smaller Wormwood were doing everything that they could do, short of shutting down the bank. "Are you sure that you still want to go, Geoffrey?"

""Yes, I am. More so in fact. These people don't let many things get in their way. I know precautions have been taken, but I've still got a funny feeling way down here," he said pointing at his stomach, "And before you say anything, Inspector, no it's not gas."

""Why, Mr. Cambridge," he said with complete innocence. "What in the world would give you the idea that I would say anything like that? Seriously, I have felt that gut feelings were not what they were cracked up to be; however, after watching the two of you in action, it seems that I was wrong. You must remember that in my field of expertise, it wasn't instinct, but solid scientific facts that helped solve crimes.

"Now, you two children run along and plan the trip. I'm tired, and I think I will catch a quick nap. Go on; that's right." The two professional investigators went into Samantha's room to make plans and phone calls.

"Early the next morning, after a filling breakfast, the three sleuths departed Boston by way of the John Fitzgerald Expressway. As they got near the New Charles Dam, the expressway turned into I-93. They got off the interstate two exits later and drove in a northwesterly direction on Highway 54. This was a wide, well kept two lane state highway that meandered past farmlands, fields of wheat and barley, pastures of sheep and cows, and even an occasional small town. About an hour later, according to the map, the road made a sweeping tum so that it was now going in an east, west direction. Thirty minutes later, they had to reduce their speed as they entered the City of Smaller Wormwood.

"Just after they passed the city limits sign, they noticed that a street sign designated the road as it went through town, as Enclosure Avenue. On both sides of this four-lane avenue, there were a number of residential areas. The outermost ones were newer, with more modem structures. However, as they traveled on towards a hill and the downtown area that could now be seen in the distance, the houses became older. They found out later that these houses were as old as the ones that were located in Sturbridge, Massachusetts. The streets in this area were all lined with trees and the homes all had quite a bit of landscaping. The streets that branched off of the avenue ran in a north, south direction, the cro:5s streets in an east, west direction, much like streets in all towns. There was one exception to this and that was another wide street that forked off to the right. It was called Continuous Ridge Road, and it went through town in a sweeping curve and out into the county.

"They drove slowly on, taking in the sights. Ulnar pointed out the hill first, noticing that the street they were on split in two up ahead. Just beyond that, on the nearside of the foot of the hill, there was a service road that connected the one-way right lanes with the one way left lanes on the other side. As they passed the 200-foot hill, they saw that the downtown businesses were on both sides of it. There was also a service road on the other end of the hill. Samantha turned left onto it. She merged with the traffic on the opposite side and drove back the other way.

""I read about this hill when I studied the map of the town. It's about a mile and a half long and as you saw, it was narrower at the ends than in the middle. There, it's about a half mile wide. The town grew up over the years around it. Originally, back in the late 1750's and early 1760's, during the French and Indian War, there was an earthen French fort on top of the hill at the eastern end. Later, during the Revolutionary War, there was a British fort there as well.

"From what I've learned, though, the British merely added onto the existing French fort. The whole hill was thickly wooded, except where they thinned out the trees. But because of the gentle slope, it wasn't easily defended. You can see the outer breastworks in places along the sides of the hill, as we pass by them. Today, the city and county offices, the Sheriff's and Police Departments, as well as the Fire Department, are all located on top. Mmm... from about the center of the hill running west. There was an aerial picture taken of it some years back. It showed four modem buildings not more than two stories high, each. This road I'm turning onto will take us to the Smaller Wormwood Police Department". The road to the top meandered gently through the woods. At the very top, signs directed people to the places they wanted to go. The building that housed the Smaller Wormwood Police Department was straight ahead.

"She parked their car and walked through the entrance of the unusual, two-story building. They followed the hallway to the right, which led to the Police Department. The left hand hallway lead to the Fire Department. They took the elevator to the second floor. This was where the administrative, records, and identification divisions had their offices. The jail was on the first floor. They walked to the office of the Chief of Police. They were ushered into his office where he came around his desk and greeted them.

""Good morning. I'm Chief Stephen Willingham".

""Good morning, Chief, I'm Special Agent Samantha Adams, and these two gentlemen with me are Geoffrey Cambridge of the British Embassy in Washington, and Inspector Ulnar Loop, formerly of New Scotland Yard."

""An honor to meet all of you. I understand that you think that our local branch of the Paul Revere Bank will get hit again. Well, we've done everything that we can ... extra patrols, an undercover officer in the bank to help with the security, and two extra security guards for a total of four. Not much else we can do for now; although, I don't really believe that they will hit it again. They can't be that stupid. They must realize that we'll be ready for them."

""That may be true, sir," Samantha answered, "But the one thing these people are not, is stupid. They are ruthless, and their history suggests that they do not take failure lightly. They will be back. You have our guarantee on that, Chief."

"He let the subject drop and told them that he would introduce them to the crime scene and latent print people. They went down the hall to a locked door. "For security," the chief said. "You'd be surprised at the number of civilians who will just walk through any unlocked door, regardless of what it said, and into an office that they didn't belong in."

"They walked into a room full of activity. There were three people in the room. Two of them were hovered over numerous pieces of glass. Slowly and with a great deal of purpose, they were processing them with powder much the same way that Samantha did at the bank. Right before one of the people was ready to photograph and lift one of the latent impressions, she took just a little more powder and applied it to the latent by brushing the powder in the same direction as the ridges were flowing and not in circular movement that the other was using. "Inspector," Geoffrey whispered, 'It's been a long time, so could you tell me why that person is dusting the latent like that? In the same direction as the ridges are flowing?"

""She wants to bring that latent out a bit more, to make it clearer for comparison purposes. A circular motion is used because you don't know what type of pattern or part of the hand is going to show at first. Once it's brought out and you want to make it darker, you apply the powder to the ridges in the direction that they are flowing. To do otherwise is to risk destroying the evidence."

"They watched in silence as the crime scene technicians finished the work. The third person in the room was at a desk talking to someone on the phone. " ... you want to be real careful printing that man. He's been known to bite and scratch when he's in that condition. Uh huh, that's right. The best thing to do is to let him sleep it off and print him when he's sobered up. You'll get a better set of prints that way." He hung up just as a woman in her thirties came out of the next room.

""What was that about, Dusty?" She asked.

""That, Fingers," he said pointing to the phone, 'Was a problem in taking some prints down in the jail. Our old friend with an explosive temper is back. Again."

""Oh, no. Not Terrence Nathan Thomas. What's this, the fourth time in as many months?"

""That's right, dear. Except this time, he's gone and committed felony assault on his wife, not the normal third degree, what the law calls domestic violence. Of course, if the courts would do their job right and either get that clown some help, or put him away for awhile, then this wouldn't have happened." He thought for a moment and then sadly sighed, "Maybe."

"The Chief of Police interrupted, "Excuse me, everyone. I'd like you to meet our distinguished guests. This is Special Agent Samantha Adams of the FBI, Mr. Cambridge from the British Embassy, and Inspector Loop, formerly of New Scotland Yard." He said gesturing at them with his left hand.

""The two people on the right doing something with glass," he shrugged, "are Crime Scene Technicians Gina Evans, and Rodger Royce. The man at the desk is Sergeant Peter Whorl, also a Crime Scene Technician. To his right, the woman that he was talking to, is his wife, Cynthia Loop-Whorl. She's our I.D. Supervisor and Senior Latent Examiner."

""Wait a moment, sir." Ulnar said to the Chief. "Ms. Loop-Whorl, aren't you actually a Certified Latent Print Examiner?"

"She looked startled. What was this man, a mind reader, she thought to herself? "Why yes, Mr. Loop, I am. How on earth did you know?"

""Not long after my retirement, I had an old friend from the Yard down at my cottage for a visit. He was a member of the Fingerprint Society, in Britain, as well as a member of the International Association for Identification. He brought a volume of that organization's forensic journal with him. It seems that on a page that named newly made Certified Latent Print Examiners, there was a strange name. It was Cynthia Loop-Whorl; the name was so close to a fingerprint pattern called the Central Pocket Loop Whorl, that we found it quite amazing.

"Chief," he continued, 'You should be very honored to have this person working for you. Do you have any idea the amount of education, training, and experience a person needs to be able to take that test? Let alone, pass it? Why out of all of the latent print people in America, only about 800 are certified. Yes, indeed sir, very proud."

"Cynthia could not help herself. A smile that stretched from ear to ear formed on her face, and she beamed.

"The chief said, "Oh, yes. Of course, I was aware of that. Well, I'll leave our visitors in your capable hands Sergeant." He turned and left the room without saying another word.

"Peter motioned to everyone in the room to gather around. Then they all went up to the three law enforcement specialists and shook hands. Cynthia spoke up. "Welcome to the bifurcation station." Everyone stopped and looked at her. The Inspector suddenly started to laugh.

"Geoffrey and Samantha stood there silently wondering what had happened to Ulnar. Finally, after a minute or so, he got himself under control. Wiping the tears of laughter from his eyes, he said, "Well done, young lady. Bifurcation station! Oh, that was lovely," he said holding his stomach.

"Geoff turned to him and asked, "What's so funny, Inspector? I'm sorry, but Samantha and I don't get the joke."

""Ahem, um, well!" he exclaimed, still trying to catch his breath. "We walked into this building through a single entrance. Then two hallways broke off evenly in two different directions or forking away from each other like a fork in the road. A bifurcation is a word used in fingerprints to describe a single fingerprint ridge that splits, forming two separate ridges."

""Ah, yes. I see," said Geoffrey. Ulnar knew that he didn't really see. So, he let the subject drop and changed the topic.

""May we see your operation, here?"

""Certainly, sir." Peter Whorl replied. Before we start, would anyone like some coffee? We have some fresh brewed, right over there. And of course, every policeman's favorite. Fresh doughnuts." He added, pointing to the far wall. They politely declined.

""This is the crime scene office and lab area, such as it is. Here, all of the evidence from a major crime scene that can be moved, such as burglary, robbery, rape, or murder is brought. That is, if it can be processed with powder, fumed with superglue, or its some tape that needs processing on both sides. Anything else that needs chemical treatment such as iodine fuming for fats and oils, ninhydrin for ammino acids, or even some of the newer ones that fluoresce under laser or alternate light sources, must be taken to the state lab on the other side of town.

"Although next month, we'll be able to use the first two chemicals that I mentioned. By then we'll have a fuming chamber on that wall over on the left, where you see the hole in the ceiling for the exhaust vent. Oh, and we do have a black light for use with some chemicals, such as Ardrox or Rhodomine, that attach to superglue. We have increased the amount of latent impressions of sufficient ridge detail with that combination. By the standards that you are used to, we know that this isn't much. But it's more than we've had before. We keep pushing for more and one day it may happen.

"Um, Cindy? Why don't you show our guests the fingerprint section."

""This way, please," she said as she ushered them through a doorway into an adjoining room. "We all share this office space. Our two Fingerprint Examiners that you see classify, search, and compare the inked fingerprint cards that were sent down from the jail with cards from the inked fingerprint, or ten print, cards that we have on file.

My desk is over there next to the latent print files. Those files are kept in order by case number. Quite often there are no suspects on these cases, so cold searches are done against the known inked prints that are not only in the ten print files, but also in the major case print files that have been built up over the years. With any luck an identification is sometimes made."

"You mean that you don't have any of the new technology, such as the Automated Fingerprint Identification System (AFIS)?" asked Ulnar. "That would cut down on the time that is used for searching so that more cases could be compared, and identifications possibly made against your local criminal element. It would also be of great help in your ten-print searching, too."

"We know that sir. But, again, the money is not available; not even for an imaging system that would help to enhance borderline latent impressions that are turned into this office.

She thought a minute, "Well, that's not quite true. The jail has a live scan fingerprinting system which has helped them take better prints. · Of course, the detention officers have worked very hard to take the best possible inked prints. Now they can do it even better.

As far as grant money, with very few exceptions, there's not much of that around for law enforcement agencies either. It's not just here; it's a national problem. If the politicians don't cut some funds, then we're sunk, as far as using the new technologies in fighting crime."

Sergeant Whorl spoke up then, "Would you care to join us for lunch? It's just about that time." He said looking at his watch. "There's a cafeteria downstairs, and I thought that it would be a nice idea if we ate outside at the tables that are set up."

When everyone had bought their lunches and were seated at a well-kept table, the sergeant went on to explain that many of the employees ate there when the weather was cooperative. It was well shaded and at the same time very open and pleasant. The woods had been thinned out and a large amount of landscaping had been done to make the entire hill a pleasant park for people to either ride bikes, walk, or even jog on the numerous paths which covered the entire top of the hill. This had been started two years before the bi-centennial and completed three days before the 200th anniversary of this country's independence from the British.

"And," his wife, Cynthia, continued, "It paid off for the city. At first, the residents were about ready to string the mayor and the city council up from the nearest unthreatened species of tree. Well, that is, until they found out that they would gain more revenue from the tourist trade. They even voted for the extra money to fix up the forts and the outer lying defensive positions for the occasion."

Geoffrey spoke up, "It's apparent that they did a splendid job of making this a pleasant park. In fact, I'd say that it comes close to rivaling some of the older, more established parks in London."

Samantha agreed. "There are a lot of people in D.C. that could take lessons from whoever designed this park. By the way, does it have a name?"

One of the two Fingerprint Examiners, Hank Haldeman, spoke up. "The city held a contest to name it right after it was finished. The winning, or most common suggestion, was French Fort Hill. But the local wits call it 'The Grassy knoll'."

"Is there a hotel in this city that you would recommend?" Asked Agent Adams.

Peter said yes, there was an excellent, well-known, hotel not four blocks from where they were sitting. He told them that when they drove back down the road they came up on, to turn left and take the second right. That was South Maple Drive. Two short blocks later on the right they would see the building. "It's one of the best hotels in the city," he added.

After everyone finished lunch, the trio made their apologies and left for the hotel. For the rest of that day, and the following two days, they found the location of the bank in question so that they could see for themselves, the level of security. The three of them entered the bank and checked out the human and electronic types of security that were being used. They also noted the number of times, and the regularity of those times, that a marked squad car passed by so that they could make a report. For the most part the precautions were found to be more than adequate. However, a change had to be made with the police in the way that the marked squad cars made their rounds; they were too regular. Samantha also had the camera angles changed so that more of the teller area was covered. Other than those two small problems, no other faults could be found with the arrangements. The news from Boston broke on the afternoon of their third day in Smaller Wormwood.

For the first time since they had been in Smaller Wormwood, Samantha's room phone rang. That alone sent the three of them rushing towards it. Sam reached it first. "Hello?"

"Samantha? This is Bill Williams. I've got some really good news; we've identified four out of the six people that we believe were involved in the bank jobs. The composites from the computer programs as well as the finger and palmprints have arrived. So far there are four matches of composites to photographs with the Irish Terrorists' packets that were sent to the Hoover Building. Because of that, Director Dickinson has asked for more possible names of the people that ran around with John Flynn and Liam Mahr. We've sent the inked prints over to the senior latent examiner at the Boston Police Department. With any luck, we'll hear something by tomorrow sometime."

"That is great news, Bill. What about the stiff in the morgue"

"Nothing yet. I've been told that his prints will be compared right after the latent palmprint from the bank has been compared to all of the inked palmprints that were sent over here from the Royal Ulster Constabulary in Dublin."

"Just a minute, Bill. Geoff? ... Geoffrey has something to ask. What is it, Mr. Cambridge?" Mr. Cambridge told her. "He wants to know whether or not they sent pictures and prints on Martin Dunn, Kevin McCarthy, Brian O'Keefe, Sean Flaherty, or Corey O'Brien." He says that they are known associates of John Flynn and Liam Mahr."

Bill checked the list of names that he had received. "O'Brien and Flaherty are not here. The others are. Does he really believe that these two may be here also?"

Sam asked Geoff, and he said yes. She told Agent Williams. "Okay, I'll send for them right now. With what's been happening on these bank jobs, I think that they will be here by tomorrow morning. I'll let you know if we get anything else."

"One more thing, Bill. Have there been any leads as to who dumped the body in the dumpster."

'Nothing yet, Samantha. The police are out talking to their sources. Of course, when you're dealing with those people, it takes time and patience. I'll call if anything else comes up. Stay in touch, please." He hung up.

Sam filled Geoffrey and the Inspector in on what was going on. She also told them that by tomorrow, or at the latest the day after, they may have their questions answered about the robbers. After she finished with the report, she said, "Well, gentlemen, I'm starving. Who's going to take me to dinner?" Not surprisingly, Geoffrey won the honor.

Saturday morning, two days later, Samantha knocked on the adjoining door. The Inspector answered from the other side. "Come in, come in, Samantha. Would you care for some breakfast," he asked pointing to the wheeled cart full of food.

"Well, if you don't mind my nibbling on some bacon, I'll take you up on the offer." Geoff and Ulnar moved their chairs. After which Geoff got up and got another one for her and held it for her while she sat down.

She looked over the food to see what there was to eat. The wonderful smell of all the food got to her; she gave in and loaded up a plate. Geoff and the Inspector grinned at each other. "Not hungry, are you?" Geoff asked with a straight face.

With an equally straight face, she replied, "No, you should see the plates I fill up when I am."

"And still manage to keep your girlish figure. My, my." He finished.

She blushed. When she recovered, she asked, "What do you intend to do today, Inspector?"

"I hadn't planned on anything specific; although, I have been thinking of going out for a walk. Yesterday was too damp and dreary. I've already checked the forecast this morning, and today, or at least this morning and early afternoon, are supposed to be perfect. Besides, I'm really tired of the indoor life that I've been leading lately. You two moles, living so much of your lives in offices. You should get out more and enjoy the fresh air." He said, forgetting about all of the hours that he spent inside when he was working for a living.

Samantha didn't bother answering him; instead, she said, "I thought that might be the case, Inspector. So I took it upon myself to make a phone call just before I came over here. In the next hour or so we, or I should say you, are going to have a couple of guests." She held up her hand to stop any protest that might have been forming. "Now, hear me out. You know that we don't want anything to happen to you. Granted there have been no new attempts on your life, and we want to keep it that way.

There is also the fact that Geoff and I must stay by the phone in case anything breaks on the robberies. We wanted someone with you, but at the same time did not have a bodyguard. So, I've invited a couple of people to join you in your walk that you might enjoy talking to. And no, I'm not going to spoil the surprise. You'll just have to wait." She smiled at Geoffrey. It wasn't often that someone pulled the rug out from Ulnar Loop.

Fifty minutes later, there was a knock on the door. No one else made a move to answer, so the Inspector got up and opened it. At first, he just stood there looking, not moving. The surprise was complete. Then, breaking the spell was Geoff's voice. He said, "Well, are you just going to stand there, sir, or are you going to show that we British do have manners?"

"I'm terribly sorry. Do come in, please." Cynthia Loop-Whorl and her husband, Peter, walked onto the room. Ulnar pointed at some chairs and invited them to sit down.

"Samantha was just telling me that you didn't mind taking a walk with an old man."

"No, sir. Not a bit. In fact, it gives us a nice chance to pick your brain and find out what it was like working in the Science of Fingerprints in the early years."

"And pick up some great tips on how we might improve our little operation." Cynthia added.

Ulnar looked at Geoffrey Cambridge, who simply shrugged his shoulders. He turned back around to his guests and said, "Yes, I would be delighted to answer your questions. In the meantime, I may also find out what it is that made you two choose these two unappreciated scientific fields that you are working in."

They said their goodbyes to Sam and Geoff and left. The walk started out as a tour of the southern end of the business district. Half an hour later, without any thought to it, the trio headed for French Fort Hill and its walking paths.

During the next two hours, Cindy and Peter asked Ulnar about his past. They talked about his parents, Merlin, and Morgana, and what it must have been like to work with, and later for, Sir Edward Richard Henry. He told them about this man who brought a very workable fingerprint classification system to Scotland Yard. "And of course, later, the science was introduced into the United States."

"Oh, yes. That's right," Cindy said. "That was done by Sergeant John Ferrier of Scotland Yard in 1904 at the St. Louis World's Fair." Wasn't he also there to protect the crown jewels that were on display at the fair."

''Exactly. Originally, he taught the science to five people, including women. And from there it spread throughout your entire country. In fact, a funny story came out of that introduction. It seems that there was a man in that city, at the time, who said that he was a very rich lord ... or something. His name escapes me right now ... but they used his fingerprints as an example of how the system worked. The prints were sent to the Yard and when the results came back, it was determined that he was really a con man. He had the entire upper crust of that city completely bamboozled."

''I remember now. Ahh, the power of fingerprints." She said.

Peter added, "And stupid crooks. They help make our jobs so much simpler." He looked at his watch. "Good grief, look at the time. Inspector, I'm terribly sorry to keep you walking all of this time. How about we take a break."

"That's an excellent idea, young man. You two have certainly kept me walking and talking until I am exhausted. Don't tell that to Geoff and Samantha, though. They might want to know your secret. Where to?"

"Over there, at that vendor's cart. He has the best foot longs that money can buy."

"What? Footlongs?"

Peter said, "Sorry sir. Foot longs, two words. They're a type of hot dog. Tastes great on a day like today. Especially with everything on it."

''Honey," Cindy said, softly stroking her husband's arm, "Inspector Loop might not want to try something like that. He may want something a little closer to what he would normally eat."

"No, that's quite all right. I would love to try one of your foot longs with everything on it". They bought their meals and found a nice bench in the shade to enjoy them.

While the crime scene and fingerprint specialists were eating their meals, there was a person in Boston who wasn't eating. She was Philipa Gnomer, the Senior Latent Examiner for the Boston Police Department. And at this very moment she was comparing the latent palmprint from the bank robbery in Sommerset with the inked palmprints of Sean Flaherty and Corey O'Brien. She was just finishing the comparison of O'Brien's palms with the latent when her boss walked into the latent unit.

"How are you making out, Philipa?" He asked.

"No match yet, Lieutenant." She said as she put her hands in the small of her back and stretched. "Phew, this does get to the back after awhile. I'm going to start comparing Flaherty's right palm next."

Being a non-fingerprint person himself, he didn't know how she could tell which palm she was looking at. So, to help him see what she was looking at, Miss Gnomer took the latent palmprint and put it into the comparison machine which enlarged it so that he could see without looking through a magnifying glass. She pointed out the area of the palm that had enough ridge detail for comparison.

"What you're looking at here, is the Hypothenar area of the palm," she said as she pointed out that area of the hand. He looked at her in confusion. "That's the large meaty side of the palm below the little finger. Now, the area that the thumb is hooked to, is called the Thenar." She pointed to that side of the palm. "Although that side of the palm is slightly smeared on this latent, and not good enough for comparison purposes, you can still see how the ridges form a large semicircle ... add to that, these horizontal creases at the top of this side of the palm. It's because of the flow of these ridges along with the creases on the hand, that I can usually tell, not only which palm I may be looking at, but also which part of it I'm looking at." She pointed each of these overall palmar characteristics out as she talked about them. Philipa walked back to her desk and retrieved Sean Flaherty's inked right palmprint.

''Now,'' she said after she had put the inked print onto the other side of the comparator, "As you can see, I've got the same areas of the two prints showing. Actually, I prefer to do this with my magnifier, but it's easier to show you how I'm making this comparison by using this machine.

The first thing that I look for is what is called a ridge grouping. That's where there are usually three or more ridge characteristics that are right together. And to me, they are something that I can easily find on the other print. In this case, I have these two ridge endings with that dot between them." She pointed these three characteristics out to him. ''Now I'm going over to the inked print and look for the same grouping." Very carefully, row by row of ridges, she looked for her ridge grouping. "There. There it is; see? Now I go back to the latent impression and count up two ridges and go slightly to the left. There I see a ridge forking, or bifurcation, to the left with another one directly above it forking to the right." She went back to the inked print and counted up two ridges and went slightly to the left. The same two ridge characteristics were there.

"I now have five matching characteristics. In other words, they are the same type of characteristic, and they are in the exact same place in relationship to one another on both prints."

"In other words, you're saying that the prints are the same." The Lieutenant said.

''No, sir at least not yet. I have to compare all of the characteristics on the latent with the ones on the inked print. When I'm finished doing that, and they are all the same types of characteristics and are in the same place in relationship with one another, with no dissimilarities, then I will form my opinion. And only then." Philipa emphasized.

"Oh," was all her supervisor could say. ''Whatever. When you're finished and you think they're the same, write up your report and give me a copy. The Commissioner wants to send it over to the feds as soon as possible." He got up from the comparison machine, turned around and left. How do they do that day after day, he thought to himself I'd be either blind or driven buggy doing that. He sighed. Oh well, better them than me.

When he left, she took the prints out of the machine and went over to her desk with them and sat down. After she had readjusted her desk light, she took her magnifying glass and put it back on the latent impression. She started her comparison again.

Twenty minutes later, she completed her examination. There were forty-seven matching ridge characteristics with no dissimilarities. Her conclusion was exactly what it should be with all of that evidence. The two prints were identical. She put the latent aside, after making her notes for her report, and reached over to the other side of the desk and got the post-mortem prints that she had taken from the body that had been found in the dumpster. She started comparing that right palmprint with the one that she had identified with the latent print from the bank.

About a half an hour later, she formed her conclusion on that comparison. They to, were identical. After another hour of writing up her reports, Miss Gnomer took them to her boss. He thanked her and told her to go on home. When she had left, he called the Commissioner, who in tum called Bill Williams at the FBI Field Office.

Bill, after he hung up the phone from that conversation, called the Hoover Building and gave his report to Special Assistant Director Melvin A Noma. "Yes, sir. I'm going to fax the reports to you. That's right, sir. At least we have positive proof of at least one person who was involved in the robberies. Now all we have to do is find them. I will; I will, sir. Oh, don't you worry; you'll be the first to know when we locate them. The Boston Police have men out checking their street sources. Something is bound to tum up real soon ... uh huh, right... thank you again, sir. Goodbye." Next, he called up Samantha with the good news.

After the call from Bill Williams, she went into Geoff's room. He was in an easy chair reading a detective novel. "I wish it was that easy with real crimes." He said to her when she came into the room.

''How about some good news; in fact, let's get the car and pick up the Inspector.''

''Now?'' Geoffrey asked.

''Now. That way I can tell you both at the same time.'' They left the hotel.

They drove around the southern side of the downtown area. Not finding him there, and knowing how he enjoyed seeing the different types of landscaping, they drove up to French Fort Hill. As they went into the public parking area, they saw Ulnar with the Whorls. They were corning from one of the many paths that go to the part of the hill where the forts were located. Samantha honked the horn and waved at them. The three walkers went over to the car. The Inspector looked tired, but happy.

"Since all of you are here, I'll tell all of you the good news." She related the facts that Agent Williams had given her about the identification of the latent and post-mortem prints.

"That's great," Cynthia Loop-Whorl said.

Geoffrey was even happier. ''I knew that that piece of garbage would end up where he did. In with the garbage.'' They stared unbelievingly at him. He saw this and explained. ''Back a few years ago, I was on assignment to Northern Ireland. There had been a series of nasty bombings. All of them are bad, of course, but these were worse on purpose. This one gang of scum that was suspected of the bombings, had among its membership, one Sean Flaherty. Regardless of how ruthless they did their work; he would go out of his way to hurt the victims again. He didn't even have to know them. He would wait around sometimes to see if anyone survived the bomb, and then he would walk right up to that person and kill him, or her for that matter.

One time, after a bombing, he was caught killing someone in that manner. When he was asked why, he told them that he wasn't known to that person. So, no one could point a finger at him. That was his way of saying that he had no regard for human life; that he just liked to hurt people.''

Peter Whorl asked, "Why is, or was that is, he still around? Didn't they put him in prison for the rest of his life for that murder?"

"Of course, he was. But after serving only five years of the sentence, Sean was able to escape. No one has seen him until now. In fact, no one even knew where he was. Thank goodness that the others in his brigade finally got fed up with his antics, and hopefully, your FBI, or the police, will find that one person who will have seen his so-called comrades dump the body."

"If, they haven't left the country," Cindy said.

Geoff replied, "No, they haven't. Not yet anyways. Remember they have some unfinished business in your fair city. And", he emphasized, "I'd bet a month's pay that they are going to strike any day, now."

"I don't see how with all the precautions we've taken at the bank. Why, they'd be foolish to try." Cynthia said, still doubting.

"There's one thing that these scums aren't-- and that's foolish," Ulnar said, "And yes, you've done just about everything that you can do to legally protect the bank. However, that will not stop these people at all. They don't know the meaning of quit, and they don't like to leave unfinished business behind."

That took some of the happiness out of the day for everyone. Sam said, "Can we drive you back to your place, Mr. and Mrs. Whorl?"

Peter said, "That would be nice of you. We left our car back at your hotel. And since there is still some daylight left, and my wife won't let me forget, I have my honey do list to work on."

"Okay, then. Everybody hop in." Sam said.

Ulnar knew what his statement had done. So, he said, "Why don't you let Geoff or me drive, Samantha? You do, of course, realize that we both have current driver's licenses."

"I would, if you two would drive on the correct side of the road. More accidents happen here in the states because of English drivers. If either of you got behind the wheel, why there's no telling how many elderly ladies you might take out. No, I think we will be safer if I do the driving."

The next day, Sunday, was again a beautiful New England summer day. After the three sleuths had gotten around and had breakfast, Samantha suggested that they go into Boston that afternoon and catch a ball game. She was a Red Sox fan, and the team was playing at home against the Yankees. "That sounds like an excellent idea, Samantha. I've been over here for quite awhile and have come to like the game. Inspector?"

"Well, I've never seen one" said Ulnar, "Although, I have heard that they are interesting. I've also heard that they are very confusing."

"Don't worry, sir," Geoffrey said, puffing up his chest, "I'll explain the whole thing to you as it's being played. You won't have a problem with it at all."

They went to Fenway Park in Boston and had a wonderful time. Ulnar didn't understand that much of the game, and Geoffrey's explanations left something to be desired. But he still had fun and even caught a foul ball. Of course, it did drop right into his lap. Boston won 4 to 3 in extra innings. Sam liked that. It meant that the Red Sox were still in the hunt for the playoffs. On the way back to Smaller Wormwood, the sky began to get cloudy.

CHAPTER EIGHT

"Monday morning arrived with a sky that was still overcast, and the threat of some severe thunderstorms was in the air. The weatherman confirmed this feeling and also predicted that the front that was responsible for the weather would be around for at least two more days. That was the first of the bad news. Ulnar received a call from Peter Whorl. The Paul Revere Bank of Smaller Wormwood had been robbed.

"Geoffrey, Samantha, and Ulnar arrived at the police department on French Fort Hill some twenty-five minutes later. Cindy went down to escort them up to the Latent Print Unit. She told them to the best of her knowledge, what had happened.

"When the tellers and the other people who work at the bank arrived at 7:30 this morning to get ready for the 8 AM. opening, they were met with an open safe."

Samantha asked, "How much moncy is missing?"

"They don't know yet. When Peter called to tell me about it, the investigators and top bank examiners were still going over the books. It will be awhile until they have an exact figure. Whatever it is, it will be a lot. Probably more than they've gotten from any of the other banks. From what I've heard and read, they never took the time to hit a safe at any of the other heists."

''You're right about that, "Sam said. "What about the bank president, isn't he the only one who can open the safe? I assume, since you made no mention of any signs of an explosion, that they didn't blow it open."

"That's right on both counts. The president of the bank is the only one who can open the safe, and there were no signs of a forced entry into it." Cindy thought for a moment, "Hmm... I wonder what Mr. Monies, he's the president, had to say about that little fact? I'll call Peter and see if he's heard anything more."

She got Peter on a cellular phone. "I don't like to use the radio when I talk about a case. Too many ears ... Peter? Listen, I was just talking to our visitors about the robbery. What did Mr. Monies have to say about the safe? Uh huh, uh huh. No where to be found? Do you think anything has happened to him...? Okay, I'll tell them.

Peter says that the bank president is nowhere to be found. In fact, no one has seen him since Saturday morning. Some of the tellers go to the same church that he and his family do. They say that he never misses a Sunday; unless he's very ill. No one saw them yesterday ... "

''Not even then?" Geoffrey interrupted. "Are they sure ... hmm, yes, they would be." He started to pace the floor, talking to himself "Family, you say? Children, too?"

Cindy who was slightly startled by this outburst, said, "Family? Why yes, there is. Two boys and a gi ... "

Suddenly Geoffrey stopped and snapped his fingers, which interrupted her, "Of course! It has to be!"

"What has to be," Ulnar asked. He looked into Geoff's eyes, and his mouth snapped shut. Then he opened it again and said, "You're right. That's exactly what garbage like them would do."

''Would somebody mind filling me in? I'm sorry, but you lost me. What do children have to do with the bank ... oh, no." Cynthia added softly.

Samantha called the Boston Field Office and spoke to SAC Williams. "Bill, they hit the branch bank of the Paul Revere Bank here in Smaller Wormwood. The police are on the scene and have everything under control."

"Okay, Sam. Thanks for the call. Is there anything special that you need?"

"No, sir. Everything is okay. I just wanted you to be aware that they hit again. We'll keep you informed on any results as soon as we get them." She hung up and turned around to face Cynthia Loop-Whorl. "How long will it take to get to your Mr. Monies home?" She asked hurriedly.

"From here, without lights or siren, maybe fifteen minutes. But before we leave, let me contact the crime scene people at the bank." She called Peter at the bank and told him where they were going and that he needed to send someone over there, fast.

Cynthia drove the visitors to the banker's home in an unmarked car. She did not use the siren. Fearing that by doing so, she might give something away. The news about the banker would get out soon enough. There was no use giving anything away any sooner than was necessary.

When they arrived, there were no other law enforcement people there. Samantha ordered Cindy and Ulnar to stay in the car. Geoff stayed behind to make sure nothing happened to them. Sam carefully crossed the front yard up to the house; she looked into one of the living room windows. There were five people in there, tied up. She went back to the car, drove it one block away, and waited until the police arrived. She told three of the first five officers to arrive at the scene, "There doesn't appear to be anyone else around, so you three go around and cover the back." She pointed at the next two and said, "You two come with me." When the first three officers were in position in the back of the house, Sam and the other two officers positioned themselves on either side of the front door.

"FBI! Come out with your hands up," she shouted loudly. Silence. There didn't seem to be any movement or noise coming from inside the house. She looked at the two men with her. "You," she said pointing to the larger of the two, "On the count of three kick in the door. I'll go lower and left. You two go high and to the right. Okay. Ready? One, two, three ... " The door smashed into and dented the wall behind it with the force of the kick that it was given. The three of them went in with their guns extended out in front of them; their eyes darting around the room, looking for anything or anyone that did not belong. It was clear.

They cautiously went through the house room by room. When the house was secure, they called in the three from the back of the house. "The family's in the living room," Samantha said.

Mr. and Mrs. Monies were in two of the dining room chairs. The children were on the sofa. All five of the hostages had their mouths gagged with duct tape; it also had been used to bind their hands and feet. Sam asked one of the officers to go to the car and tell the three people there to come into the house.

''Don't touch those bindings yet." She warned the officers. "I know that they're uncomfortable, but we don't want to damage any possible evidence. Mr. and Mrs. Monies, I'm sorry about this, but I don't dare to remove the tape and possibly ruin any fingerprint evidence that might be on it. The only way that we're going to be able to put these people away is on good, solid, fingerprint evidence. The crime scene people will be here in a matter of minutes, and they will be able to remove the tape.

"And," she added, ''We'll have paramedics standing by to help you, after you've been freed from your bonds." She called the police dispatcher on her cellular phone to take care of that matter.

Sam posted one of the officers outside the door to keep all unauthorized people from entering the house, and to keep a list of all who did enter. The other officers were to start canvassing the neighbors' houses. These men would start the gathering of information until the investigators came to take over. This information had to be noted before it became too old and people forgot anything that they might have seen.

As Samantha gave out her instructions to the officers, Peter Whorl and one of his crime scene people arrived. The other one, Gina Evans, had been left at the bank with an officer trained in crime scene procedures, to finish the collection of evidence from that scene.

"Go right on in," the two of them were told by the officer at the door. He jotted down the date, time, and both of their names onto his list. Peter and Gina quietly and quickly, with no wasted movements or words, set out their equipment. She started taking pictures of the overall crime scene, which included where everyone was sitting. This also showed that everyone was taped up. When Gina was finished, she and Peter started to remove the tape from each victim, carefully labeling each piece before it was transported to their makeshift lab. This included the date/time, victim's name, case number, and from whom the tape was removed. Other notes were made as necessary.

It was during this time that Sam, Cindy, Ulnar, and Geoff left for the police station. There was no need for them to be at the scene; they would just be in the way. When the four of them arrived at the station, Samantha called the Boston Field Office and requested that they get copies of the suspects' major case prints to Smaller Wormwood as fast as possible.

At the banker's house, he and his family had been freed of their bonds, and the paramedics were waiting for them. They were transported to the hospital as a John Doe to begin the treatment that would eventually allow them to get over this experience. Of course, the physical part of the treatment would be the easiest. The psychological wounds would take much longer. Investigators would meet the family at the hospital, so that a bond between the police and the victim could be formed. This way a great deal of information could be gathered at the beginning, in a very short period of time. Other sessions would be scheduled for later dates; after the mental injury from the ordeal had started to settle and more details might slowly arise.

Peter Whorl and Gina Evans took the tape back to the Crime Scene Unit. He handled the tape very carefully so as to avoid leaving his own prints on the sticky and non-sticky sides. While they were engaged in getting the tape ready for processing, Rodger Royce returned with the latent impressions that were photographed and lifted from the bank. He would log this evidence in and finish filling out the necessary information on each latent lift card from his notes. After which, he would write out his complete report for the case.

Two specially trained investigators were at this moment taking elimination prints from each of the bank employees. Afterwards, they would go to the hospital to obtain elimination prints from the Monies for comparison with any latent prints found at their home, as well as the bank. The cleaning crew that came into the bank during the week would also be printed. When the current batch of physical evidence had been properly logged in, Gina and Rodger left the office and returned to the banker's house. That scene had not been disturbed by anyone. They entered, with their names noted by the officer at the door and started processing any item that appeared to have been touched by the offenders.

Back at police headquarters, Peter and his wife were starting to process the duct tape that had been removed from the victims just as a police officer, who was acting as a runner, delivered the first sets of elimination prints. Cindy took them into her unit and had the two latent examiners, Hank Haldeman and Marlon David Plaites, compare them with the latent impressions from the bank.

Peter and Cindy placed the tape that was used on Mrs. Monies in the small fish aquarium that was used for iodine and superglue fuming. When the pieces were in place, a few drops of superglue were placed on a flattened-out cotton ball that had been dipped into another chemical. This would react to the glue and produce white fumes. A light bulb was inside the tank through a hole on one side. The heat from it would speed up the fuming process. They placed a snug fitting lid onto the top of the tank.

The fumes could be seen rising up towards the tape. After approximately eight minutes, prints started to show on the non-sticky side of some of the pieces. They waited a few more minutes so that the prints could develop fully. At the same time, they didn't want to destroy the latent images because of over fuming. A small vent hood over the tank was turned on, and the lid was removed. They stood back until all of the fumes were removed and then carefully took the pieces of tape out of the aquarium.

The white latent prints stood out on the gray of the duct tape. They were photographed with a special fingerprint camera. After the film was developed, Cynthia took the photos into her office and started to compare them with the inked finger and palmprints of the Irish suspects which had arrived just as the first pieces of tape were being fumed.

In the crime scene room, Peter was starting to put the next series of tape into the fuming tank. The Inspector was standing off to one side watching this young man do the work of two people and couldn't help but think that yes, there are still professionals in the field. Even in a small city police department like this one. Peter called over to him, "Inspector? I was wondering if you could help me for awhile".

"Certainly, Sergeant Whorl. What is it that you would have me do?"

"It's Peter, and you could fume and photograph the rest of the tape for me while I take the finished pieces and process the sticky side of them."

"Of course ... Peter, I would be honored to help." He started the fuming process for the second time. At the same time, Peter started to mix a photo chemical, water, and black graphite powder into a thin paste that looked about as thick as paint. He took a camel hairbrush and painted this mixture onto the sticky side of the tape. He allowed it to dry for a few seconds and then rinsed it off with slow running water in the sink. He did this with each piece of tape that had been processed and photographed on the opposite side.

It would be a long afternoon and evening by the time they finished with all of the tape. It would be even longer for Cindy and the other two examiners. There was a lot of latent evidence to sort through and compare.

Geoffrey and Samantha were watching them do just that. Cynthia took her magnifying glass and set it down on the first photo to determine if there was enough ridge detail. She went through the entire set of pictures, setting some off to her right and others off to her left. The first pile were the latents that she would be working with. All of the others were of no value for comparison purposes.

The first latent was that of a fingertip. Or the area of the finger just above the pattern on the finger and below the nail. She started with the inked fingerprints of Kevin McCarthy and worked her way through his tips. Next, she selected Brian O' Keefe's prints. In both cases she started with the left thumb because of the size of the latent print and the slope of the ridges. Both of these factors suggested that it might be that finger.

Cindy had already studied the latent impression and found her ridge grouping. It consisted of an enclosure, skipping one ridge upward there was a ridge ending to the left, and skipping another ridge upward, there was a ridge forking, or bifurcating, to the left. She went over to the approximate area on the inked left thumb print of Brian O' Keefe. After a minute or so, she found her grouping. She went back to the latent; the ridge immediately above the forking ridge was a ridge ending to the left. Back to the inked print and there was the same characteristic. She continued going back and forth between the two prints until she had compared every ridge characteristic on the latent print. The opinion that she formed at this time was that the two prints were identical.

"How are you making out?" Asked Samantha.

"Well, I found the first one, but it's going to be a long day. See what I mean?" Cindy said pointing to the door as Peter walked through it with more photos of latents developed from both sides of the tape. "What did I tell you. Hi, slave driver; more work for us I see."

"You didn't expect to get off with just a couple of easy comparisons, did you? If I've got to work, so don't you."

When he turned his back to leave the room, she stuck out her tongue at him and made a raspberry noise. He turned around and gave her a juicy one right back, and left. Four hours later, he was still working on his reports. The other two crime scene people were doing the same.

In the Latent Print Unit, with the remains of a takeout dinner scattered around them, Cindy and her crew were still comparing the latent images of sufficient ridge detail from the two scenes. Geoff and Samantha were still watching them. The Inspector was sitting in a comer trying to stay awake. It had been a number of months since he had done such demanding work. Peter came in from his office, 'I've sent my people home for the night; maybe you should do the same, hon."

She looked up from her work, stretched her arms above her head, and yawned. "What time is it anyways?"

"It's after nine."

"Good grief, that late. Well, everyone, I suggest that we go home, get a good night's sleep, and start in again at eight when we're a lot fresher." No one argued.

The next morning was still overcast and threatening rain when Peter and Cynthia got to their offices and started the coffee. They also put out some donuts for their people who came struggling in at about 7:30. By 8 a.m. though, with their bodies fortified with sugar and caffeine, they were ready to finish the two cases.

Peter, Gina, and Rodger completed their paperwork three hours later. While Sergeant Whorl went over their paperwork, Evans and Royce were called out to take care of three residential burglaries and two auto thefts. As he was completing that chore, Geoffrey, Samantha, and Ulnar were escorted into the office by the Chief '" Morning, sir. What can we do for you?" He asked his superior while waving at the three visitors and gesturing at the coffee.

The Chief watched the three of them go over to the coffee pot. "Are you finished with your reports yet?"

''No sir, not yet. Well, mine are done and I've checked the others' reports and they're ready to go. If you're asking about the latent print reports, then I don't know anything about those, sir; you'll have to check with Cindy.''

''No, that's alright. When she's done, have her submit them to my office. The press got their hands on at least part of the story. Someone at the hospital talked. Right now, we have the Monies family under protective custody. They will continue to get the medical help they need while they are in that position. So, with the news people having part of the story, they're now clamoring for more information. You know how they can be.''

"That I do, sir. I'll tell her when she's done. Although, you know that no matter who wants it and how fast they want it, she won't release anything or write a report until she's positive that the prints either match or they don't match. But for now, here are copies of all of our reports." He handed them over to the Chief.

"Thank you, Sergeant Whorl." He turned and left the room.

Pete looked over at Sam, and said, ''Why don't you three go on in. I know that Cindy would love to see you. And I believe that she has some more news on the identifications.'' They didn't need to be told twice.

All of the examiners were busy writing reports. Cynthia Loop-Whorl looked up, smiled, and waved the three sleuths to some chairs. ''Well, we've completed our comparisons. In a nutshell, the bank had no prints that belonged to the suspects. They were mostly the president's and the other employees; that also included the cleaning crew. Five prints remain from that case, but from the location of them, they could belong to any of the bank patrons. However, the house is a different matter. She looked over at Marlon Plaites.

''M.D.?''

"Right. Well, Agent Adams, we ended up with about sixteen prints from both sides of the duct tape. Nine of those were of sufficient ridge detail for comparison purposes. Of those, four belonged to Brian O' Keefe, including the one that was identified last night. The other five belonged to Martin Dunn ... "

''Him?" Geoffrey interrupted. ''He's here in the states? Oh, there are a number of law enforcement agencies that would like to get their hands on him. Although, he has said that he will never be taken alive. Remember when we found out about the guns; well, that's his type of operation. I'd like to be around when they catch up with that piece of scum. Yes," he said in a low voice to himself, "This family was very lucky to be alive. After all, the type of people that you are dealing with are more used to random murder by the use of explosives. These people are not used to robbing banks, or just holding hostages the way that they just did. I'm sorry, sir; please go on with what you were saying."

"Some of the other prints from the house were from the kitchen and bathroom," Marlon continued. They were located in places that would be normally touched. Such as the refrigerator, the counter around the sink, plates, and silverware. We picked up Kevin McCarthy's prints in this area. It looked like he must have prepared some of the food that was eaten. That's just about it, Agent Adams."

''Excellent. Cindy, you and the other two examiners did an outstanding job. I'm going to include your names on the list of people that I've already started for special recognition for your dedication and professionalism in these two cases; along with a number of your officers and investigators. By the way, that includes the three people in the next room. You've all earned it." She got to her feet. "I'm also going to call Bill Williams at the Boston office and give him the rundown on the names that we have through the fingerprints. That way, the people in Boston can get copies of the pictures of this slime and show them to the public. Especially, the area surrounding the dumpster where they found Flynn. With any luck, maybe we'll be able to close these cases by the end of the week. If, that is, they're still in town." She raised an eyebrow and looked at Geoffrey Cambridge when she said this. The others noticed something else in that look.

"Yes, I believe that they are still in the area." He looked at the local examiners and said, "We've already gotten a preliminary report on what happened to the Monies at their home. These fools haven't changed their act a bit. They wore the same costumes that they've worn throughout their crime spree. Apparently, they like the look. Or, maybe even thought that the costumes may have some sort of luck attached to them. For whatever reason, they didn't change th ... "

"Hooray for stupid crooks," Peter said from behind them. Everyone was so interested in what was being said that no one had heard him enter. "By the way hon, the Chief wants your reports as soon as possible. It seems that the news people have gotten wind of what has happened, and he needs to make them happy. Apparently, someone at the hospital talked out of tum."

"That's just great. I hope that he doesn't give to much away, you know, like the names of the suspects."

Samantha said, "He won't. I'll have Bill Williams take care of that."

"Come in, young man, come in," Ulnar said. "You are one of the main reasons for our being here today and getting all of this good news."

"Thank you, sir, I believe I will." He went over and pulled up a chair next to his wife.

"Please continue, Mr. Cambridge," the Inspector said.

"Ladies and gentlemen, to put it simply, I don't think that they have left town, yet. They just made their biggest score, and as has already been brought out, they weren't in this alone. They may still have to pay someone off for helping them plan these jobs. And, more importantly, the weapons that they are to buy will have to be paid for in this country, then shipped to the northern counties on one of the many cargo ships that travel between Russia, the Middle East, and Northern Ireland. No, they're still here, and we've got a good chance at finding them.

"Thank you, Geoff," Samantha said, "I'll pass that along to Bill Williams with the rest of the information. May I use your computer, first," she asked Cynthia.

"Of course. Help yourself"

Samantha Adams sat down at the keyboard and started to write the report from her notes that she would be sending by special delivery, to the Hoover Building in Washington, D.C. This would include everything from what was handled by the local police to Geoffrey Cambridge's remarks about how the scum would operate. As well as to why they would still be in the area. Her recommendations for the thank you letters that the bureau would need to send out to certain individuals would also be included in that report. Two hours later she finished the document and faxed it to D.C. Then she called Special Agent Williams in Boston.

The phone rang a number of times. Then the receiver was picked up, and a voice said, "FBI, Agent Williams speaking; may I help you?"

"Bill, this is Sam; and yes, you can ... well not help us ... but, instead, help yourselves; along with the local police agencies. We have some names for you to pull, along with their pictures. And you'll need to get those mug shots out in a hurry before they go back to Ireland. Are you ready to copy?"

"Yeah, just a minute ... okay I'm ready. Go ahead."

Samantha said, "The robbers, or at least three of them, have been identified. I'm going to fax you a copy of the crime scene and latent print reports. Another copy is going to be faxed to S.A.D. Melvin Noma for the Director. I'm also sending a special delivery package to him by mail. The names are Brian O' Keefe, Sean Flaherty, and Martin Dunn. But watch out for this group. According to Mr. Cambridge, they are a particularly nasty bunch of hardcore bombers; especially, that Dunn character. He is reputed to have said that he will not be taken alive."

"Okay, Sam. I have that... anything else?"

"Just a couple of things, if you don't mind. First, the Chief up here might spill the beans to the press if we're not careful. Seems that they got some information from the hospital, and he's going to give them some quotes from the official reports. Oh, and then could you let us know if anything turns up? These people all deserve at least that much for all of the work that they put into the case. And very professionally, if I may say so."

"We can do that, Sam. Where will you be found?"

"We'll stay on at the hotel; however," she looked over at the Whorls who were motioning to her and mouthing words. She nodded her head yes. ''However, we'll also be at the Whorl family's home for dinner during the next few nights. During the day, we'll be out taking in the sights for the Inspector, who would like to see some of the historic parts of town as well as some of the landscaping. He said that he just might use part of it for his own gardens."

"Okay, I've got it. Thanks again to everyone." He hung up the phone.

Sam passed on Agent Williams' thank you. And then she, Geoff, and Ulnar said their goodbyes and left. That way, the latent and crime scene people could finish their reports and continue on with their daily chores. They drove back to their hotel after having a pleasant lunch at a local diner.

That night after dinner, Geoffrey took a walk to the nearest phone booth. He attached the electronic device to the speaker and dialed a special direct number. In London, Commander Cummings picked up his phone.

"Cummings, here."

"Good evening, sir, Geoffrey Cambridge here. I've got some good news for you."

"Oh?"

"Yes sir. They've identified the robbers. Or at least three of them. A fourth one is dead; his own mates did him in. The leader is Martin

Dunn. The other two are Brian O' Keefe and Kevin McCarthy. And, I might add, there may be more. Right now, though, no one is certain how many."

"Excellent. You will let me know when, and if, they are captured, Mr. Cambridge."

"I will, sir."

"By the way, why did you call me in this manner? Were you uncertain how far the current cooperation might extend?"

"Let us say, sir, that I wanted you to know what has happened without any unnecessary delay."

"I see. Well, thank you again, and be careful. Goodbye."

Geoffrey went back to the hotel room. He had a good night's sleep.

By the next day, the rain had stopped although, it was still overcast. The three visitors went for a drive around and through the town and the historic districts. Even in this damp, dreary weather with the water dripping off of the trees and other shrubs, the greens and reds, browns, blues, and all of the other dull and bright shades of color, stood out in a brilliant work of art. As the week wore on, the weather, and their spirits improved. The three of them drove around the City of Smaller Wormwood, and later on, the surrounding countryside, to see the many different versions of New England landscaping. Each night they would stop by Peter and Cynthia's house which lay on the outskirts of the city. It was a small, neat Cape Cod that sat on an acre and a half of land, much of which was wooded. The grand tour was given that first night.

It started on the top level of the home, which was the second floor. This was made up of two bedrooms and a den. It was here that Peter and Cynthia kept their professional books and the Journal of Forensic Identification (this was a bimonthly booklet dealing with special topics such as: firearm, fingerprint, tire tread, and handwriting identification, etc.). First, they showed their guests the two bedrooms and the den/

computer room. On the ground floor, there was the eat-in kitchen, mud room, and living room. But beneath those rooms lay the cleanest room in the house, the basement.

The basement stairs descended down along the North wall from the kitchen; the washer/dryer combination and furnace were located along the opposite wall. The furnace was near the wall directly in front of them. To the right of the dryer was a door leading into another room.

"This is our pride and joy", Peter said. "Cindy and I work together in this room to help educate ourselves in processing crime scenes. You can see a PVC pipe leading out of the wall up there," he said as he stretched his arm upwards and pointed up to a spot just below the ceiling. "That's for the small vent fan; so that we can work with some of the many chemicals without harming ourselves. As you can see, there's also a small darkroom set up on your left. This is where I come, to not only develop crime scene practice photography but to work on my photography hobby."

Geoffrey spoke for everyone when he said, "Sergeant Whorl, I congratulate you on being a very thorough and complete professional ... "

"But, when's dinner?" asked the Inspector.

There were sometimes that a person wished to shoot him. Maybe it wasn't such a good idea to help him become what he was before his retirement, Geoffrey thought. Out loud, he said, "That sounds like an excellent idea, Inspector."

Two nights later, on Friday night, Ulnar suggested that the five of them go to dinner as his guests. As usual, no one said, no. "After all, if the Inspector invites anyone out to a meal, take advantage of it," Geoffrey said. "It may be a long time before this happens again."

"Are you saying that I am cheap, and that I only invite people out to eat at my expense on a very rare occasion?"

"Yes." Geoffrey said simply.

"Hrumph!" the Inspector exclaimed in mock anger.

The phone rang. "It could be work," Cindy said, reaching for the phone. "Hello?" It wasn't.

"This is Bill Williams calling from the Boston Field Office. Is Samantha Adams available?"

"Yes, she is; just a minute, please." Cynthia handed the phone to Sam.

"Yes?"

"This is Bill. Are you near a television?"

Agent Adams looked over at the Whorls. "Do you have a television handy?"

Peter said, "We do. Why?"

"Turn it on to the local CBS station, that would be WBZB out of Boston." That is all he said.

"Okay, thanks," Sam said. She hung up the phone. "Turn it on to WBZB; apparently there's something going on that we're supposed to watch." Peter went into the den and turned on the set.

" .. ing. I'm Priscilla Purity."

"And I'm Morton Moronne. The top story in our news tonight is the continuing stand off of an unknown number of armed men holed up in a hotel in the southern part of our fair city. We now go to our correspondent on the scene, Dimh Lyte; Dimh?"

"Yes," Dimh said as she held up her left hand to her ear to hold the earpiece in place. "There has been a standoff between elements of the local FBI, members of our own Boston Police Department, the Bureau of Alcohol Tobacco and Firearms (BATF), and what you have mentioned as an unknown number of men. This standoff started at approximately 1:00 p.m. this afternoon when elements of these law enforcement agencies tried to serve warrants on the occupants of Room 325 at the Broken Arms Hotel. That's the building you see directly behind me."

"Excuse me, a moment, Dimh. Why is the Bureau of Alcohol, Tobacco, and Firearms here, if they are bank robbery suspects?" Asked Purity.

"According to official sources, the suspects may have automatic weapons that were smuggled into the United States by foreign gangsters. These weapons were to be smuggled out of this country and into Ireland, this according to a high-ranking source in the police department."

"Just a minute." Dimh saw Agent Antoine Martin who was the head of this federal and local task force. "Is there anything that you can tell us at this time, Agent Martin? Could you tell our viewers what you're planning to do?"

"No comment."

"As you can see, the police are not answering any questions. However, I did find out earlier from a source who is familiar with this siege, that the law enforcement agencies had already removed the people that were in the surrounding rooms. So, the suspects cannot take any hostages. The combined agencies also called in a negotiator to try and get the accused out without having to go in using force. But it does look to this reporter that that is exactly what they would like t... "

Suddenly, there were two sounds, like someone coughing. Poom, poom. Then the sound of breaking glass. The reporter turned around to see just in time, smoke billowing out of the broken window. "It looks like they're going to use that force after all." She was cut off by other sounds.

Through the broken window came the sound of a door being forcibly opened and hitting a wall. There was shouting along with several shots ... then silence. Dimh Lyte started to rush forward so that she could have a better look. A policeman stepped in front of her and stopped her.

"That's as close as you get," he said to her. "Any closer and I'll have to arrest you for interfering with an officer."

In the background the television viewers could see more police and federal agents rushing into the building. Fifteen minutes later, three men came out with their hands above their heads. Actually, only two had their hands up; the third was holding his shoulder with his other hand. Police and federal agents were beside each of the suspects, as well as in front and in back of them. Others came out a few minutes later carrying several automatic weapons as well as a field mortar. While things were still calming down, and the tear gas was thinning out, Dimh Lyte heard an amplified voice say that a press conference was going to be held across the street in ten minutes. She and her camera man rushed over so that they could get a good spot up front.

"Ladies and gentlemen of the press. There have been many rumors going around about what has been happening for the last six hours. So, I have a brief statement to make. I will not take any questions afterwards. Those will be answered in due time at Police Headquarters.

This arrest procedure started at 1300 hours this afternoon, when agents from the two federal agencies that you saw here, and the Boston Police Department, arrived at the Broken Arms Hotel to serve warrants for the arrest of Martin Dunn, Kevin McCarthy, Brian O' Keefe, and Sean Flaherty. They were reported to be staying here by other sources.

Upon arrival, law enforcement agents knocked on the door of room 325 and announced themselves only to be fired on by the suspects. The residents of the hotel in the surrounding rooms were quietly taken out of the hotel. A police negotiator was called in to get the four men to surrender without the use of force. However, after six hours this was not going to happen and the decision was made to storm the rooms, at which time one of the suspects was killed, one was wounded, and one of the BATF agents was slightly wounded. The suspects are going to be taken to federal court in the morning to be arraigned on robbery, murder, and hostage charges. The government in Great Britain is being notified at this time1 also.

These men are wanted for dozens of murders as well as terrorist acts in Great Britain. As to who will try them first, that will be up to London and Washington. As I said earlier, further statements will be forthcoming from Police Headquarters. Good day."

"Well, as you can see, Priscilla and Morton, this crisis has ended but there are many unanswered questions. Back to you." Dimh finished.

"That was certainly something to see," said Priscilla. "Coming up nex ... "

Peter shut the television off. "I believe that our troubles that were caused by that slime are now over."

"It certainly seems so." Samantha Adams said. "What are you going to do now, Geoffrey?"

"That depends on the Inspector. I will have to continue to escort him around if he decides to stay in your country. However, that would now be a rather pleasant task."

Ulnar spoke up, "Thank you Geoff. In fact, thank you all. Agent Adams, for your concern and your help in saving my life and helping me to understand that I may be retired, but I am certainly not dead. Also, that I still have much to give to people. To Peter and Cynthia for letting me see that professionalism, no matter the size of the agency, is still alive and well. It is a refreshing change from the attitudes of these so-called professionals that I see when I go out these days." He turned around. "Geoffrey, my new friend, I don't know where to start ... "

"Then don't, sir. Where is it that you would now prefer to go." Geoffrey said in a soft, caring voice.

"Home ... yes, home .. " Ulnar said in an equally soft voice. "I've been away so much longer than I had planned for; not by me of course, but the powers hat brought me here. My garden and my home, they beckon me." In a livelier voice, he said, "But right now, let us go to the dinner that I promised you. There is much to celebrate and to be happy for, now." It turned out to be a very wonderful evening.

The next morning, Geoffrey and Samantha drove Inspector Ulnar Loop to Logan Airport in Boston. While they waited for the plane, Cindy and Peter showed up. When it came time for the Inspector to board the flight, there was not a dry eye among them. As they watched the plane taxi out to the runway, Cynthia Loop-Whorl said, "He's such a nice gentleman, a good, kind man. I wish I had known him longer." She slipped her arm through her husband's and looked at him with a tender, caring look on her face and said, "He's only the second one that I have found in my entire life."

Samantha looked sideways at Geoffrey, so that no one would notice, and said, "I couldn't agree with you more, Cynthia."

They stood there in silence while the plane waited for its tum at the end of the runway. The four new friends watched it take off. Then slowly, sadly, although richer for this new friendship, they walked back to their cars and to the rest of their lives.

CHAPTER NINE

""Two months later, on a chilly, overcast afternoon at Twinned Loop, the Inspector was just returning from a brisk afternoon walk that he told people helped his digestive tract. Actually, he just liked the exercise, and it gave him a chance to talk to his neighbors. If they were outside. As he left Ridge Ending Lane and walked up the graveled driveway, he heard the faint ringing of his phone. He looked at his watch. ''Now who on earth could that be," he muttered to himself.

"He got out his key to the front door and let himself in, hoping that the phone would keep ringing until he could answer it. Hurriedly, he turned left and walked into the library where his adventure first started. There on the table where Constable Correy had sat drinking tea, was the phone. It was sitting next to a beautiful floral arrangement from his new greenhouse. He picked up the phone.

""'Hello?"

""'Hello, Inspector, Geoffrey Cambridge, here. How are you these days, sir?"

""'Splendid, Geoffrey, just splendid," he said as he saw a small buff colored envelope leaning up against the flowers. He picked it up and opened it. ''What is the news over there?" A small piece of stationary, the same color as the envelope, slid out and dropped onto the table.

"Well, the two governments have decided on how to handle the three robbers that were caught in Boston and the one who tried to ruin your day in New York. It seems that America will have the first go at them. When those sentences are served, they will be sent to England to stand trial there. After all, there is no statute of limitations on murder."

The Inspector rested the receiver between his ear and his shoulder. He picked up the folded piece of paper, unfolded it, and started to read as he said, "And how is that Agent Adams doing, or don't you keep in touch?"

"As a matter of fact, sir ... " Ulnar heard no more. His eyes were glued to the paper in his hand.

My Dear Inspector Loop,

"You have stopped my plans many times now. You have even escaped your own death, twice just recently. I will not allow this state of affairs to continue unchecked. Therefore, I have decided to put a stop to this foolishness the next time our paths cross.

With Sincerest Regards
Professor Radius

ASSISTANT TO INSPECTOR LOOP